I0522944

BILLY WHISTLER

*The Bayou Hauntings
Book Four*

Bill Thompson

Published by
Ascendente Books
Dallas, Texas

This is a work of fiction. The events and characters described herein are imaginary and any reference to specific places or living persons is incidental. The opinions expressed in this manuscript are solely the opinions of the author. The author has represented and warranted full ownership and/or legal rights to publish all the materials in this book.
Billy Whistler: The Bayou Hauntings 4
All Rights Reserved
Copyright © 2019
V.1.0
This book may not be reproduced, transmitted or stored in whole or in part by any means, including graphic, electronic or mechanical without the express written consent of the author except in the case of brief quotations embodied in critical articles and reviews.
Published by Ascendente Books
ISBN 978-09992503-2-7
Printed in the United States of America

Books by Bill Thompson

The Bayou Hauntings
CALLIE
FORGOTTEN MEN
THE NURSERY
BILLY WHISTLER

Brian Sadler Archaeological Mystery Series
THE BETHLEHEM SCROLL
ANCIENT: A SEARCH FOR THE LOST CITY
OF THE MAYAS
THE STRANGEST THING
THE BONES IN THE PIT
ORDER OF SUCCESSION
THE BLACK CROSS
TEMPLE

Apocalyptic Fiction
THE OUTCASTS

The Crypt Trilogy
THE RELIC OF THE KING
THE CRYPT OF THE ANCIENTS
GHOST TRAIN

Middle Grade Fiction
THE LEGEND OF GUNNERS COVE

Dedication

This book is dedicated to the wonderful people of Abbeville, Louisiana. I visited Vermilion Parish doing research for this book, and fell in love with its Southern charm and beauty. Everywhere I turned, friendly people helped me. I got tips on haunted houses, unusual sites in the parish and whether Dupuy's or Shuck's had the best food. The jury's still out on that one – I loved them both!

Many of the places I visited when researching *Billy Whistler* resulted from conversations with Abbeville locals. I went to Perry, Bancker Grotto, Henry, Esther and the cemetery at Mouton Cove. I stopped to watch a crawfish farmer in an airboat running his traps and I saw a lot of the beautiful Vermilion River, which plays an important part in this story.

Thanks to you wonderful people who helped me so much. I'll be back — now that I've visited Vermilion Parish I can't stay away!

Acknowledgments

Special thanks go to Carolyn, Gretchen and Natalie at the Caldwell House, a wonderful old mansion I highly recommend for an overnight visit. While I was there, I also met Carolyn's sassy and captivating granddaughter Ava. She and Carolyn have roles in this book.

My research began in the parish court clerk's office, where Nanette was a huge help. Tip is one of the security people at the courthouse, and I appreciate his patience as I went back and forth. They're in the story too.

Thanks to Lee and Brent, two local folks I was fortunate to sit beside at the bar at Shuck's. They gave me insight about local lakes and Vermilion Bay. The man at the cultural center, whose name I'm sorry I failed to get, gave me lots of useful information about the town of Perry. Many others offered tips and advice.

I also appreciate my old friend, former District Judge Tom Landrith, who furnished helpful legal information.

CHAPTER ONE

The night of May 26, 1880

Abbeville, Vermilion Parish, Louisiana

The Fleur de Lis Tavern faced Pere Megret Street near the river. It was a melting pot for the lower end of society — stevedores from the dock, former soldiers still grousing about a war the South should have won, free men of color, merchants, and a few females — working girls rotated in from Baton Rouge to serve the customers.

As a clock chimed ten, five men gathered around a table in a storage room at the back of the tavern. On a mission, each slipped in through the rear door and crept along a dark hallway to the meeting place. If someone recognized them — and in this small town it could happen — their plans would be thwarted.

The men were there to rid Vermilion Parish of a pestilence. For years a cult called the Sons of Jehovah had lived near the river south of Abbeville. They built a commune, which they called Asher, after a biblical king of that name. Even the word *commune* made the good

Catholics of Abbeville blush. That word sounded like fornication, and people whispered that that sin — and a lot worse — was going on out there in the woods.

The only practical way to get to Asher was by boat, and people snuck down there now and then to see what was going on. They reported hearing plenty of whooping and hollering, accompanied by loud hymn-singing 'til the wee hours. To some, it sounded just like the all-night revivals the Pentecostals held every year outside town, but no one dared suggest the sacrilege of a cult compared to legitimate prayer meetings that God-fearing Christians conducted.

A courageous spy ventured down late one night and barely escaped with his life. As he rowed away, they spotted him and launched several boats. Only by hiding in the trees along the shoreline, he related later in his breathless account, did he escape capture and certain execution in some crazed ritual. Thank God he made it back to tell the others what was happening in that abominable hellhole. His report sounded awful: they seemed to all be drunk, jumping around, speaking in tongues, and all naked as a jaybird, and — this was the worst part — some of the naked ones were young girls not even developed yet.

This was the last straw. From the pulpit next Sunday morning the town priest said they might call themselves the Sons of Jehovah, but Jehovah played no part in what those despicable sinners were doing. Sons of Lucifer was a more fitting name, and something must be done. God demanded it.

Perhaps the spy's account had been true, or maybe he invented it to get the ball rolling. True or not, from then on the festering issue of Asher was all people talked about. Men from the cult were easily identifiable in their black suits and tall stovepipe hats. When they came to town to buy supplies, people glared at them and crossed the street to avoid passing too close. Some shopkeepers ordered the men to leave, saying their kind wasn't welcome. Over evening meals, wives asked husbands why no one did anything, and at last five men decided it was time.

They came from very different backgrounds, and only something like the outrage at Asher would bring them together. Besides being in their thirties and Abbeville natives, they had just one thing in common — each of them was a regular at the Fleur de Lis, and each was outspoken about his disgust over the Sons of Jehovah.

Frank Cocheron made his living cutting and selling timber. He hired a crew to fell the trees, used a team and wagon to transport logs to the dock at Perry, and sold his load to merchants who hauled the logs in boats down to the Gulf. Frank worked long hours doing backbreaking work and lived in a shack down by the river. The only he spent was on his sole frivolity, drinking whisky at the Fleur de Lis every evening.

David Hebert served as Abbeville's first and only funeral director, and his business was picking up, even though many people still preferred to hold services at home. He and his wife lived in a nice two-story house and were well off in comparison to most.

Bobby St. John was the parish sheriff by day and a regular at the Fleur de Lis by night. He drank too much, and as a result he was always broke. That infuriated his wife, who struggled to raise four children with no help from Bobby.

Simon Navarro did a little of this and a little of that. He was a smuggler and rumrunner on the Vermilion River, a frequent patron of the ladies of the night, and a hard-drinking renegade. He was at the bar every night and often ended up on the sidewalk outside when his mouth and the liquor ended him in a punch-throwing brawl.

Auguste Dauphin worked in one of Perry's many blacksmith shops. Street-smart and handy, he carried a chip on his shoulder. Auguste blamed the world for his situation, his lack of formal education, and most anything else that dealt misfortune to him. He was strong and his black beard and mustache gave him a fierce countenance. When Simon Navarro got in a fight at the Fleur de Lis, Auguste always jumped in too. He didn't care who won — he just loved to fight, bully and push people around. His father had died in a tavern gunfight when Auguste was a little boy. He left him an 1844 ten-dollar gold coin with the initials AWD carved into it, and Auguste carried it in his pocket. He called it his lucky piece, although it had brought no luck to father or son.

The proprietor allowed the men to use his storeroom for their clandestine meetings. He knew what they were up to, but he didn't ask questions. There was a blasphemous scourge in the parish, and maybe they'd fix it. The priest had said God wanted this done, and that made it all right.

After too many drinks one evening, they agreed on a plan. Over the next few days things came together, and at the stroke of midnight on May 26 — tonight — they would settle things in Asher.

The five sat in the back room, knocking back shot after shot to bolster their courage. The night before at eleven, Simon had taken his boat down to Asher. He'd watched and listened and found everything dark and quiet, and that was what they needed to know. Folks went to bed before midnight in Asher.

When the clock struck twelve, they raised their glasses in a final toast, walked down to the river, and loaded several canisters of gasoline onto two boats. They pulled away from the dock and the mission was underway. Although there had been plenty of alcohol already, each carried more whisky to fortify himself for the task that lay ahead. They swigged from their flasks and sat in silence as the boats floated down the Vermilion, the only sound the swish-swishing of their oars.

CHAPTER TWO

Present Day

After a quick lunch at one of his favorite French Quarter restaurants, a place called Kingfish, Landry Drake walked to Royal, took a right, and entered the studios of Channel Nine — WCCY, the Voice of the Crescent City.

He went to his office, tossed his jacket in a chair, and noticed a sticky note atop a stack of papers sitting in the middle of his desk.

Check this out and get with me. I skimmed it and it looks right up your alley. There's a voicemail you should hear too. Ted

Ted Carpenter had been the station manager for four years. During that time, Landry's investigative reporting segments had propelled Channel Nine into the national spotlight. The suits at Triboro Media in Chattanooga who owned WCCY-TV made what became a very profitable decision. They aired the *Bayou Hauntings* series on the company's twelve other stations. His ghost-hunting activities fascinated the public, and the popular show became a national sensation. Wherever Landry went these days, people recognized him.

Ted lived vicariously through Landry, passing along things he read or saw online that might lead to a story. The stuff he gave Landry today was a six-week series that ran in the *Abbeville Meridional* newspaper in May and June 1890. The first article was entitled "Vermilion's Dirty Little Secret: Murder, Mystery and Mayhem in Asher." Another title read "The Curious Tale of Billy Whistler: Myth or Reality?"

He procrastinated. Whenever he glanced at the pile of articles, he wondered if he would waste a lot of time wading through them. When he left for lunch, Ted caught him in the lobby.

"I haven't heard from you. Did you see what I left on your desk?"

Landry promised he'd get into it after lunch. "Those articles are from 1890," he added. "Is there something in particular I should focus on?"

"I got a voicemail, a strange one that made me nervous. Because of it, I searched the web and found what I left you. I skimmed through parts of it and sent it right over to you."

"Who left the voicemail?"

"I don't know. She didn't leave her name or a number. Usually people who call a TV station want publicity, but this one's different. I think she's scared. If you have a minute, let me play it for you before you go out."

He heard a young voice — maybe a teenaged girl — who spoke in the same syrupy drawl as Landry. She was an Acadian — a south Louisiana Cajun — and seemingly uneducated.

You don't know me, but there's bad stuff going on over here in Vermilion Parish, and somebody has to check it out. Look up the story of Billy Whistler. It ain't a made-up tale, and the cult ain't gone. Somebody still dies at Asher every Remembering Day. I'm dead too if they find out I called you, but it has to stop.

Landry listened a second time and asked Ted's opinion about what the girl said.

"Read the stuff I left you. I just glanced at it, but on the first few pages I saw references to Asher and a cult called the Sons of Jehovah."

"Yeah, and I glanced at a title about Billy Whistler. What's that about? It's a story from 1890. What's happening today that's part of something that old?"

"Maybe nothing, but I can't get that girl's voice out of my head. Do you agree she sounded scared? I want you to read that stuff, tell me what you think, and let me know if you should go up there and look around."

Landry agreed it was a thought-provoking message, but he thought Ted was moving too fast. His boss hadn't read the document, yet he was eager for Landry to go check things out. That wasn't the way the world of paranormal investigation worked. Every lead required hours of research and most of them ended up worthless. But none of that mattered this time. His boss asked him to read it, so he would.

And he had to admit something about this sounded interesting.

He changed his mind about eating out, picked up lunch, and ate at his desk. He dove into the material, taking notes and pausing now and then to search the web. He finished around five, drained after hours of research. What he learned raised more questions than answers, and the voicemail made things even more perplexing. He printed off his notes and walked to Ted's office.

Ted leaned into his desk, eager to hear what Landry learned. He said, "Give me a one-word summary."

"Puzzling. If the voicemail's true, a bunch of renegades from Abbeville started something in 1880 that's still simmering today."

"Excellent! Tell me everything — not just the facts but your thoughts and ideas. Give me the investigative angle." He leaned forward with his elbows on his desk like a dog about to get a treat.

Landry glanced at his notes. "The article is a tenth-anniversary piece recalling an event that happened the night of May 26, 1880. The Sons of Jehovah was a cult that appeared in Vermilion Parish around 1840. They bought land and built a commune on the Vermilion River south of Abbeville. They called it Asher.

"That night in 1880 some men burned the town to the ground. There were rumors that they murdered seven cult members, but there's no proof of that. One thing's for sure — the cult left their town and never returned. Maybe they disappeared, or integrated into the population, or something else happened to them. It's a mystery.

"The writer titled the article Vermilion's dirty little secret because the perpetrators were never caught, and anyone who knew anything kept his mouth shut. The writer relied on rumor as much as fact because that's all he had. Since he was a lifelong resident of Abbeville, he knew the stories as well as anyone, and that helped him build a credible account.

"One rumor was that the perpetrators lived in Abbeville, but even today no one knows for sure. The Abbeville possibility came about because the morning after the fire, a woman appeared at the office of the Abbeville newspaper — the same paper that published the articles ten years later — and reported her thirty-four-year-old husband missing. She spoke to the publisher, who also owned the paper, and said Auguste Dauphin had gone to the Fleur de Lis tavern on Pere Megret Street the previous evening around ten. He told his wife he had something important to do, and said he'd be home before daybreak, but he never returned."

The publisher said she was in the wrong place; she should be talking to the sheriff.

She shook her head and explained that her husband had been out late several nights recently. When confronted, he said he was meeting with men like him who wanted to "take care of things in Asher."

"Sheriff St. John was one of those men," she confided. "I can't go to him because I think he's involved."

The publisher faced a dilemma. He'd learned something this morning, and from this conversation, he was certain she hadn't heard it yet. Someone had burned Asher to the ground last night. Without a doubt the woman's husband was involved, and this might end up being a huge story. But he wasn't about to get mixed up in a missing person case, or get crosswise with his good friend the sheriff. Regardless of the woman's concern, and despite the chance for a scoop, this was a matter for the law.

He told Mrs. Dauphin he would help and asked her to wait in his office for a few minutes. He walked a block to the sheriff's office and repeated the woman's conversation to Bobby St. John. The sheriff also knew about the fire at Asher overnight.

"Bobby, this sounds crazy, but she believes you're involved somehow," he said, and the sheriff chuckled and shook his head.

"You and I both know Auguste," St. John said. "He drinks too much, and he talks big when he does. He doesn't have the guts to do something like that. I'm going down to Asher today, and I imagine I'll find those crazy Sons of Jehovah burned their own town and picked up stakes to go somewhere else. If you ask me, I hope it's way far from this parish. I don't need 'em."

The publisher felt better after their talk. He knew the sheriff, and he knew his friend wouldn't be part of something like that. And Bobby didn't think Auguste Dauphin was involved either. Maybe he fell into the river on his way home, or he was sleeping it off with some whore from the Fleur de Lis. He'd turn up before long.

"This is where it gets interesting," Landry told Ted.

They both returned to the publisher's office, and Sheriff St. John told the woman to come with him so they could look for Auguste. "Maybe he just got drunk last night and couldn't find his way home," he suggested, and the newspaperman would later recall that she looked anxious when the sheriff took her by the arm and escorted her out the door.

"Nobody ever saw Auguste Dauphin or his wife again," Landry said. "The newspaper guy smelled a rat, but the sheriff assured him nothing happened. He said the woman wouldn't talk to him and he sent her home. Auguste and his wife had no kids and no close friends, so for weeks nobody checked on her. When someone finally did, she had vanished.

"Since the sheriff could have been the last person to see the woman alive, the publisher was convinced that Sheriff St. John was involved, but he didn't pursue his concerns. Years later the sheriff moved away, and thanks to the newspaper publisher's habit of keeping extensive notes about everything, they became the basis for his articles ten years later. In a way they were a confession, a testimony of regret that he did nothing.

"In the voicemail the girl mentioned Remembering Day, but I couldn't find anything under that name. There's a lot online about Billy Whistler, though. He's first mentioned in 1880, soon after Asher burned. It's one of those legends that gets crazier with each retelling. And the girl's voicemail shows people think he exists today.

"Some people call him a swamp creature; others say he's a rougarou — a legendary Cajun werewolf that roams the bayous at night. He snatches helpless females and drags them off to his lair, where he ravages and maims them. He got the name because people claimed when he was near they heard an eerie whistle like a whip-poor-will's call."

Although every Cajun kid had heard the rougarou legends, Landry didn't believe the story about Billy Whistler. Most likely people who thought the cult was weird created a myth to make them scarier and more bizarre. There might be some basis for the story, but for Landry it sounded like a myth just like the rougarou.

Ted wasn't so sure. "Are you forgetting the voicemail? The girl said Billy Whistler's real."

"She said a lot of things, Ted. My job involves finding the truth, not accepting an anonymous caller's far-out claims without knowing what they're based on. This could be a joke, or a sicko, or a grudge against the cult from a long time ago. I don't know what it is, but you and I shouldn't assume anything yet."

"What'll it take to make you a believer?" Ted wanted Landry to be as intrigued as he. He could insist Landry go to Abbeville, but he hoped he'd get fired up on his own.

Landry laughed and reminded him that he often got tips on so-called mysteries. Most of them ended up explainable or downright false. Only a few merited further investigation, and ninety percent of those didn't make the final cut. The ones that did became segments in his ghost-hunting series.

"You don't pay me to believe everything," he added. "My job is to debunk the fakes and investigate the others. That said, there may be something to this story. Let's look at the facts. We have a cryptic voicemail that seems to be a cry for help. The Sons of Jehovah cult was real, their town burned, and the legend of Billy Whistler began. What he has to do with Asher, I have no idea.

"Somebody torched Asher the same night Auguste Dauphin disappeared. His wife sought help but ended up in the hands of a man she believed was part of a plot. Then she mysteriously disappeared too. It sounds like a monumental cover-up that someone has perpetuated over generations. It's almost too crazy to believe, but you know what, Ted? I agree with you. I need to go to Vermilion Parish. This may be a big hoax. If it's just a story about some crazy men burning a town a long time ago, maybe at least I can build a human-interest segment for the evening news. But maybe — just maybe — we get lucky and the caller's telling the truth."

Landry explained that the big question mark was the story about Billy Whistler. "If he's real — which I doubt — then it makes everything much more interesting, and we may have another *Bayou Hauntings* episode. I'd like to mull this over tonight and talk again in the morning."

Ted agreed, telling Landry he sure knew how to spin a story that got people's attention.

Landry left the station around six. Although it wasn't dark yet, he could already hear the tourists a block away on Bourbon — raucous laughter, cursing, horns honking, and a police whistle. *Gotta love this town,* he thought as he walked into Muriel's on Jackson Square, a frequent stop on his way home. He found its bar a quiet refuge, something rare in the French Quarter. He ordered a vodka tonic, a dozen oysters and a bowl of seafood gumbo, and he chatted with the bartender until the food came.

During dinner he got an email from Ted. "After we talked, I found another interesting story," it read. Attached was a 1921 article from the Abbeville newspaper headlined "Hunter Attacked by Rougarou."

Landry was skeptical from the first because the article didn't name the victim or witnesses. Names could be searched, relatives located, and stories confirmed. Otherwise you had just one more unverifiable tale.

Four men had been hunting one night in the woods in south Vermilion Parish. One became separated from his friends, and a creature he called a rougarou attacked him.

Its body was contorted and hairy, and it had long arms and sharp fingernails. The hunter said he sliced the creature's face and arm with his knife, escaping when his friends heard the clamor and came running, and the thing disappeared into the forest.

Landry wondered what kind of animal the hunter had encountered. The rougarous were a myth, so he figured the man saw a monkey. They weren't indigenous to Louisiana, although people said they saw monkeys from time to time. Experts believed they were pets that either got away or had been released into the wild when they became difficult to handle. What the guy thought was a rougarou was probably just a large, aggressive monkey — perhaps one with rabies.

He would have dismissed the entire story except for one sentence. The woods at night were filled with noise as birds, insects and mammals made their rounds. But this hunter heard something different — the warble of a whip-poor-will mere seconds before the creature emerged from the darkness.

The articles from 1890 said Billy Whistler had a unique warble. Forty years later a hunter reported encountering a rougarou who had the same whistle.

Coincidence? Maybe.

The stress of the day's work, the drinks and the dinner crept over him and he felt exhausted. He settled his tab, walked two blocks to his apartment on St. Philip Street, and was in bed by nine. Questions flooded his mind, and it took longer than usual to fall asleep.

He had a recurring dream, awakening him each time in a cold sweat. All he could remember was a corpse swinging from a noose in a tree.

And the eerie call of a whip-poor-will.

CHAPTER THREE

It was almost five when the dreams went away. He slept until a ringing sound jarred him awake. The phone. He popped one eye open, then the other. Rays of sunshine flooded his bedroom. He fumbled for the phone and saw Cate's name — and the time.

Nine thirty! He hadn't overslept in years. Work-wise it didn't matter because Landry dictated his own schedule, but he prided himself on being among the first to arrive at the station each morning.

He managed a sleepy hello and Cate asked why he wasn't at work. He explained and told her he'd call later. After a quick shower, he hurried over to the station.

The receptionist said Ted had been looking for him, and he stuck his head in the boss's door.

"Morning."

"Morning. Everything all right? I've been worried. I don't think I've ever beaten you to work, and I wondered if you'd already left for Abbeville."

"I had a rough night. Thanks to that stuff you made me read, I couldn't sleep!"

Ted laughed. "It got my attention too. So what's the verdict? Is it yea or nay on Vermilion Parish?"

"The article you sent last night clinched it. I'm convinced the hunter saw the creature some call Billy Whistler. It happened forty years after Asher, but there's too much similarity in the stories, so I vote a major yes on investigating this one. Now we need to find out who left the voicemail."

"I listened to the message again this morning. She sounds scared, and she wants someone to come stop bad things that are happening. It could be a prank, but my gut says it's real. She mentioned things that happened a century ago like they're still going on today. Bizarre. If you go to Abbeville, you might find out who she is."

Cate phoned during the meeting. He returned the call, but she didn't pick up. As the office manager of her father's busy psychiatric practice, she had little time to talk during the day, and he didn't bother leaving a message. She'd call when she got time.

He and Catherine Adams had known each other for just over two years. They'd shared a harrowing experience being kidnapped in an abandoned insane asylum on the Bayou Teche. They'd seen supernatural forces at work up in St. Francisville, and she supported him when his job turned dangerous now and then.

She lived in Galveston, six hours from New Orleans by car but a quick flight, and they got together as often as they could. They had discussed sharing an apartment, but his schedule was hectic and unpredictable. He might find out tomorrow he had to be in the northern part of the state for a week. Or get invited to New York for a talk show interview the next morning.

Independent and in a job she loved, Cate nixed the idea of moving. Sitting alone in a French Quarter apartment waiting for her boyfriend to breeze into town for a night or two didn't appeal to her. They lived in different places and so for now, meeting two or three times a month would be it. He'd fly to Galveston, or she'd come to New Orleans, or they'd meet somewhere fun like the beach. They thought about the future, but with Landry's increasing fame and his passion for investigating the paranormal, it might not happen for some time.

Landry put the file and his notes into a satchel and walked home. He loaded the car, crossed the Mississippi River bridge and followed highway 90 through Jefferson Parish toward New Iberia. He crossed the bayou drawbridge at Delcambre and passed men on the side of the road selling shrimp and crawfish from coolers in the back of a beat-up pickup.

For a moment he wished he'd brought an ice chest, but then he laughed at himself. Like other singles, he never fixed a meal at home. As mouth-watering as it sounded, there was no way he'd be boiling a mess of crawfish for one.

I think I'll surprise Cate sometime and throw a shrimp and crawfish boil.

Landry passed through Erath and soon came to the Abbeville city limits, where he turned off the highway toward the downtown historic district. When working on a story, he had a routine he followed in a new place. He always hit three places: the historical society, the newspaper, and the most well-established funeral home in town. Funeral directors knew more about people, places and history than anybody else.

There was something else in Abbeville that would be helpful. Being a parish seat, it had a courthouse. Parish courthouses were treasure troves of information — records that dated back to the early days, long before the Civil War.

Only twelve thousand people lived in Abbeville, but tourists often visited, and a nice cultural center sat on Magdalen Square near the old Saint Mary Magdalen Catholic Church. He spent half an hour there talking to a man who'd grown up in Perry, a town down the road that Landry intended to visit. The man said Perry had been the first parish seat and a bustling river town in the mid-1800s, with several blacksmith shops and even more bawdy houses. After a political battle long ago, Abbeville became the seat of Vermilion Parish, and Perry's population dwindled to a few hundred.

"What can you tell me about Asher?" Landry asked, and the man smiled.

"I have to confess I recognized you when you walked through the door. And I said to myself, 'Bet he's here about Asher.'"

These days everyone recognized the ghost hunter, especially here in Cajun country, where several of his *Bayou Hauntings* episodes happened. When he came to a town, everybody asked why.

"Asher's one reason I came, but it's not the only one. Do you know much about it?"

The man offered nothing Landry hadn't heard already, but he offered what turned out to be an important suggestion.

"Look up a guy in Perry named Lee Alard. He's getting old, but I hear his mind's still good, and he knows a lot about parish history. You'll learn a lot but watch he doesn't mix in a little bull with the truth!" The man looked up Alard's number and Landry thanked him for the tip.

As he left, Landry asked about restaurants, and he named two places in town, on opposite sides of the river. The oldest, Dupuy's, opened not long after the Civil War, and Shucks was its upstart rival. Locals adamantly preferred one or the other, and they'd argue over which had the most scrumptious char-grilled oysters, crawfish etouffee and okra gumbo.

"How about you?" Landry asked, and the man said hands-down he'd choose Dupuy's. Don't miss the oysters, he added. Landry left with his mouth watering, wondering if he should eat or keep working. He chose the latter.

The 1890 article Ted had shown him ran in the *Abbeville Meridional*, a newspaper which still existed. He went to their office and learned the paper's microfiche records resided at the public library but could be accessed online. That was helpful; searching online later would save time today.

Landry stopped for lunch at 1:30 because he couldn't stop thinking about those oysters. Abbeville's downtown area was compact, and people walked everywhere. He parked on the north side of the courthouse — his next destination — and walked through the square to Dupuy's. The place was busy, and he opted for a seat at the crowded bar. Over the years, he found bars were the best places to learn information. He could talk to other patrons instead of sitting alone and wasting an opportunity.

The bar occupied the middle of a large room with tables along one side. He took a seat next to a man in his forties who was washing down a plate of alligator bites with a Crying Eagle Louisiana Lager. The man said the best things on the menu were the crab cakes and the oysters. In a few minutes Landry had a beer, and soon a plate of oysters de ville arrived, followed by the flakiest, lightest and most delicious crab cakes he'd ever tasted. He left with a full stomach, a little more local lore about Billy Whistler, and a serious doubt that Shucks could outdo the experience here. Dupuy's was fun, boisterous and full of locals who obviously loved this place. He knew he'd be back, but he also had to try their rival, Shuck's.

He had to keep moving; it was after three and he had two stops left — the courthouse and the funeral home. But there was also Lee Alard. Since he was here, he should try to meet the man. He called, spoke to a caregiver named Ruby, and arranged a meeting for tomorrow morning. The courthouse closed in just over an hour; he'd knock it out and catch the funeral home on his next trip.

It was clear already that he'd be back to this quaint town. Everyone he talked to had a theory about Asher, and a few knew the Billy Whistler legend. He'd spend more time with the locals, and perhaps even learn the identity of the scared girl who left the voicemail.

Parish courthouses held scores of records, often dating back to its original settlers. But in many parishes, pre-Civil War records didn't exist today. When Union troops marched through towns in Louisiana, they often torched important buildings and destroyed priceless history. Landry had looked up this courthouse and discovered good news and bad. After surviving the War, it burned in 1885. He was looking for earlier records, and he hoped some still existed.

With its six white columns facing Magdalen Square to the west, the beautiful Greek revival building resembled an antebellum mansion. The entrance was on the north side under a beautiful New Orleans-style wrought-iron balcony. He passed through a metal detector, and a friendly officer named Tip directed him down the hall to the parish clerk of court's office.

As he walked to a counter, a friendly lady in her sixties rose from her desk and gave him a beaming smile that showed he'd been recognized. She stuck out her hand and said, "Grace Vincent, Mr. Drake. Welcome to Vermilion Parish. Ladies, look here! We have a celebrity in the house!"

Her colleagues came forward, eager to meet him and listen as she asked what brought him to Abbeville.

They all talked at once. "We're big fans, and we talk about your show all the time. Are you going to put us on television? Are you working on a story?"

He laughed. This happened so often he'd stopped keeping count. He said yes, he was here on assignment, but most things he investigated didn't end up on TV. He thanked them for being fans and asked Grace if he might see the record books for the town of Asher.

Grace gave a sly wink and whispered, "If you're looking into the Sons of Jehovah incident, you'll be disappointed. That whole thing — someone burning Asher and all — was swept under the rug in the eighteen hundreds. Even now people call it Vermilion's best-kept secret."

"Surely there will be death records. From what I hear, people died that night. Aren't those records available?"

She shook her head. "Those people were different — a cult — and they kept to themselves. I've never seen a single thing from Asher, but then again, I've never looked either. I'll show you where to look so you can see what's there. Oh, and there's one more problem. Our courthouse burned down in 1885. We still have what records they saved from before then, but it's not a lot. Some are complete and others just fragments."

Two strikes against me, Landry thought as she guided him down a hall to a long table.

"What years would you like to see?"

Since the men destroyed Asher on May 26, 1880, he asked for twelve months of records beginning with that month.

Grace brought him a large ledger titled "Burnt Records" and said he could go through the entries. If he found a listing, there would be a record. And she gave him an important bit of information he hadn't known about.

"My grandfather said everyone in that cult belonged to one of two Acadian families. Every person's last name is either Savary or Lafont. They kept to themselves and never allowed their kids to interact with outsiders. You can imagine what happened: most of them ended up related to each other because of inbreeding. Granddad said after a few generations some of them might have been so different that people thought they were rougarous."

Everywhere Landry turned, the rougarou legend came up. They were a kind of Cajun werewolf, half man and half animal, who prowled the swamps and snatched up children. They were Louisiana's answer to Bigfoot, but with a dose of malevolence thrown in.

"I'd be surprised if the parish has birth and death records for rougarous." He laughed.

She turned serious. "Like I said, it could be that people called them rougarous because they didn't know what to make of them. I think all that inbreeding took a toll on future generations."

She just might be right, he thought.

Grace left him to it and returned to work, although the clerks didn't get a lot done with a TV star in their midst. Mostly they whispered and took sly photos with their phones.

He spent over an hour, but there was nothing. He'd hoped to find death records for seven murdered cult members, but there were no reported deaths that week in the entire parish. Then he searched for records for Auguste Dauphin and his wife. Nothing. They were still unaccounted for today.

After perusing a year of birth and death entries, he gave up. There were no Savarys and no Lafonts because the cult didn't send records to the parish seat. They were reclusive and clannish, and they weren't the kind to reveal anything about themselves.

Landry called off his fruitless mission as the clerk's office was closing. He promised to visit them when he returned. That night Grace called all her friends to brag about helping the famous ghost hunter.

Neither of them knew that the assistance she gave him would earn her a visit from an irate sheriff with a bone to pick. Outsiders had no business poking around in parish secrets, or so some people believed.

CHAPTER FOUR

Landry drove two blocks north to Caldwell House, an early twentieth-century bed-and-breakfast and the first brick home in Abbeville. He always hoped to find historic B&Bs in old Southern towns, and this one promised to be very interesting. The manager had called earlier to say he'd be the only guest tonight; he'd have the entire six-bedroom mansion to himself. She left a key under the mat and said she'd drop by around cocktail hour to make sure things were good.

The minute he stepped inside he knew he'd made the right choice. The home was spacious and grand, with high ceilings, tall windows and beautiful period furnishings. His room — the master suite — sat downstairs at the front of the house off a wide entry hall. He poked around and found two more bedrooms on the first floor and three upstairs along another wide hallway.

At 5:30 Landry listened as the back door opened and a friendly lady named Darlene met him in the front parlor. She had her son and granddaughter with her. "Evie wanted to meet you, Mr. Drake," she announced as the enthusiastic girl shook his hand. "She's a huge fan of ghost hunters, and she's seen every episode of *Bayou Hauntings*!"

Ten years old, Evie was an outgoing and precocious girl with a winning personality and a big friendly smile. They talked for a few minutes about why Landry came to Abbeville, and it surprised him that even at her young age she knew about Asher and the night it burned.

"She reads everything she can get her hands on," her grandmother crowed. "She really likes history, and it's even better if there's a ghost involved."

Darlene walked him through the house, showed him where the coffee pot was, and provided a few spooky stories about the old place. She also offered to stay the night if Landry didn't feel comfortable alone in a creaky old mansion.

"I bet I already know what your answer's gonna be," she said with a grin, and he confirmed it, assuring her a night alone in a haunted mansion sounded perfect.

"It's right up his alley, Grandma," Evie said. "He's looking for ghosts!"

Once they left, Landry drove along Pere Megret Street, one of the town's oldest, and came to a drawbridge. He crossed the Vermilion River and pulled into the parking lot of Shucks, the rival dining destination to Dupuy's, where he'd had lunch. He walked into a beautiful old bar, took a stool, and ordered a Belvedere and tonic. He started a conversation with the couple next to him, and as usual they asked if he was in Abbeville to hunt ghosts.

He had an answer, one that was true but revealed nothing. He was looking into some historic stuff that had happened in the parish after the Civil War, and he was especially interested in records that had survived the courthouse fire.

These people were locals like just about everyone else there, and they wanted to tell Landry about spooky places nearby. He got his drink, and as they toasted, his phone rang. It was Cate returning his call.

He excused himself, took his drink to a nearby table, and gave her an update on his day of searching for records that didn't exist. He told her about his upcoming night in the old mansion, and that he had an interview in the morning with an old man who knew a lot of history. He'd be home tomorrow night and they could talk then.

The bar was more crowded now, but the folks he'd sat beside saved his place. They offered a couple of suggestions of not-to-be-missed sights near Abbeville. One was Mouton Cove; its cemetery was interesting because when Hurricane Rita slammed the area in 2005, rising water caused the graves to open up and caskets to float out. Things were back to normal now, but ghostly stories abounded.

The other place was Bancker, a spot near Mouton Cove that had once been a thriving community amid large plantations. A cave in the old cemetery built in the late 1800s by Acadian settlers was a replica of a French grotto dedicated to Our Lady of Lourdes.

Thinking they sounded interesting, he said he'd check them out when he came back. They chatted as he ate one of the best bowls of seafood gumbo he'd ever had — and that was saying a lot for a Cajun kid from the next parish over. He bought them a last drink, said goodbye, and walked out through the now-packed bar.

It was well after dark when Landry got back to the house, parked his car, and went inside. Light from some table lamps cast eerie shadows down the hallway and onto the stairs that led to the second floor. His bedroom was dark, and he fumbled around until he located an old lamp on the nightstand.

He climbed into the comfortable bed with his laptop and entered notes about the events of the day. His mind was buried in details when he heard a noise — a kind of thump that seemed to come from upstairs. He waited a moment, but there was nothing else. Old houses made noises; in his business he'd heard plenty of them.

Around eleven Landry sat straight up in bed. It took a moment to orient himself — he'd fallen asleep with the light on, and his laptop lay on the covers. He wondered what woke him. Was it that same sound? Looking around his room, he saw nothing out of the ordinary, so he stepped into the hallway. The lamps were still lit, but the shadows down the hall toward the stairway seemed darker and deeper now.

There was a sound, maybe a scrape, like someone was dragging something.

There it was again, coming from the second floor.

He couldn't pass up the opportunity, and he went back to the bedroom to put on his shoes, but they weren't where he thought he'd left them earlier. He looked everywhere: the closet, which he hadn't opened until now, the bathroom, and even under the bed, but he didn't see them.

That's strange. Where are they?

He heard it again. Barefooted, he walked to the end of the hall and flipped a light switch. A huge old chandelier that hung from the fourteen-foot ceiling in the hallway bathed the staircase in a soft light. Halfway up the stairs, in the middle of a tread and lined up exactly next to each other, were his shoes. He picked them up and noticed the laces were tied in bow knots. He always untied them when he took them off.

Could I have left them there and not remembered? I didn't have too much to drink, I don't sleepwalk, and I locked my door. No, it wasn't me.

He put them on and went up to a landing, with another stairway on either side. The second-floor hall was shrouded in half darkness, its only light filtering up from the downstairs chandelier. He couldn't find any wall switches, and he wished he had his phone. He stood silently, listening to the usual old-house creaks and groans. Tree branches scratched against the second-floor bedroom windows.

He opened doors and peeked into bedrooms filled with antiques. Each window was adorned with heavy curtains that extended to the floor. In two rooms they were drawn tight, and the darkness was near total. In the others the drapes were tied back, allowing outside light to filter in from State Street. The effect was surreal, like a haunted mansion on a movie set.

He gave up, returned to bed, and slept until 6:30. He turned the latch on his bedroom door and walked into the hall, heading to the dining room and a coffee pot. He glanced at the stairs and wasn't surprised to see his shoes there again. This was paranormal activity — perhaps a poltergeist — and it was exciting.

He kept his shoes in the bathroom while he showered, shaved and dressed. Even before he opened the bedroom door, he smelled something delicious wafting through the house. Darlene was in the kitchen, making cinnamon buns and frying up crisp bacon and an egg casserole.

She asked how things had gone, and he explained he'd heard thumps and scrapes from upstairs, but nothing was there. He also told her about the shoes, and she laughed.

"Nobody ever died in this house, Mr. Landry, so our ghosts aren't evil or scary. Other guests have heard bumps and thumps like you did. I've heard them too, and I think it's Mr. Caldwell moving furniture around upstairs. Come with me and I'll introduce you to him." They went in the parlor and she pointed to a portrait hanging on the wall. A stern-looking man in formal dress stared stonily ahead. "You can thank him for keeping you up," she joked.

"I think I can explain your shoes too. Mr. Caldwell had a little girl he sometimes punished by locking her in a closet under the stairway." She took him down the hall and opened a small door. Behind it was a small room lined with shelves. It was a storeroom for vacuums and brooms, but on one shelf there were dozens of dolls and teddy bears.

"Guests used to hear someone crying in that closet, so we started putting toys in there and it stopped. I'll bet that precocious little girl took your shoes and left them on her stairway where you'd find them. You didn't feel afraid, did you?"

Landry admitted to being unnerved, but no, nothing that happened was that scary.

Darlene said, "All's well that ends well, and at least you don't have to go down to the Walmart in your sock feet and buy a new pair of shoes!"

"What do you know about Asher?" he asked over breakfast and coffee, and he saw her frown just a little. She'd been outgoing and chatty to this point, but now it was different.

"Not a lot. It's been a ghost town for ages. Nobody knows much about it. There's nothing left of it and nothing to see. I can give you more interesting places to explore."

He noticed how smoothly she had manipulated the conversation away from talk of Asher.

He lingered almost an hour over coffee, listening to her fascinating stories about the house, the town and the parish. At last it was time to go. He thanked Darlene for her hospitality, loaded his car, and drove a few miles to Perry.

He really enjoyed Caldwell House and promised himself he'd stay there again. Darlene had been friendly and helpful, like everyone he met, except the two who wanted him out of the parish.

His only question about his visit with Darlene was why she wouldn't talk about Asher. Grace said it was Vermilion's best-kept secret, and maybe she was right.

CHAPTER FIVE

Perry was a tiny community just south of Abbeville on highway 82. He followed the caretaker's directions, click-clacking across another drawbridge that spanned the river and separated the two towns.

There were few streets, and Landry passed newer brick homes interspersed with old frame ones. Almost all of them were well-kept and had yards full of flowers.

He made several turns and took a dirt road that dead-ended near the river, and he came to an old three-room shotgun house perched on concrete stilts to protect it from flooding. It needed a new roof and a paint job. A rotting shrimp boat lay on its side close to the house, and Landry wondered if it had swept up off the river when Rita or Ike blew through years ago.

An old man sat in a wheelchair on the front porch, a cigarette in his hand. A black lady in a starched white uniform rocked in a swing next to him. She stood when Landry walked up the rickety stairs.

"Mr. Landry Drake! It *is* you! I recognize you from the TV. I'm Miss Ruby. Pleased to meet you, and welcome to Perry!" She flashed a broad, friendly smile and shook his hand. "This here's Mr. Lee Alard. Mr. Lee, say hello to your impo'tant guest. He came all the way up from Nawlins to see you."

Until now the old man hadn't seemed to realize Landry was there. He stared into the distance, causing Landry to wonder if he was lucid. But when the caregiver spoke, Alard jerked his head up, sending long strands of white hair flying everywhere, and looked at Landry. His bright eyes shone with excitement.

"I know what yer here for, Mr. Landry," he croaked in a voice forever altered by decades of smoking. "If yer lookin' for spooky tales, you come to the right man." He coughed violently, and Ruby helped him expectorate into a tissue. He took a long puff from the cigarette and wheezed so much Landry wondered if he had emphysema.

Ruby didn't seem concerned. She patted his back and said, "Who tipped you off that Mr. Lee could help you?"

"A man at the cultural center said Lee's forgotten more about this parish than most people will ever know. And I needed someone who could remember things going way, way back. I'm doing research and I'm hitting a lot of dead ends."

She clapped her hands together. "Research! I knew it! You're gonna do a story 'bout our parish, right? Mr. Lee and me, we'd love to be on the television." She paused, thinking she'd gone too far. "If it's okay with you, that is. I didn't mean to sound pushy."

Landry laughed and assured her it wasn't a problem. He also said it was far too early to know what might come from his research. On this trip he was looking for information about Asher.

"Which part of Asher — the rougarou or Billy Whistler?" Lee asked, his mouth twisting into a grin that revealed toothless gums. "It's always one or the other, ain't it? Ain't nothin' else about Asher that's very spooky."

"I haven't put my finger on what it is, because I'm just getting started. I'd like to know about the Sons of Jehovah and what happened the night the vigilantes burned the town. I'm hoping you know something, and if Billy Whistler's involved, I'd like to hear that too."

"Hell yes, he is," the codger snorted. He turned to Ruby and demanded another cigarette.

"Let's wait a bit, Mr. Lee. This man wants to talk to you, and if you smoke another one, you're just gonna start coughin' and you won't be able to tell him anything."

"Damn woman," he growled, although he wasn't serious; he seemed to appreciate Ruby very much. "Okay, fire away."

"May I record this?" Landry asked as he took out his phone.

The old man nodded.

"Is your full name Lee Alard?"

He sat up proudly, gave a stern glance at Ruby, and answered, "My name is Robert E. Lee Alard. I'm named for —"

She smiled and interrupted. "I think we all know who you're named for, Mr. Lee."

"How old are you?"

"A hundred and fifteen."

Ruby burst out laughing and gave him a light slap on the arm. "You old coot! You quit foolin' around right this minute. You ain't never gonna get on TV if you keep this up!" She looked at Landry. "He's ninety-seven. Born in 1922 right across the river in Abbeville, now ain't that right, Mr. Lee?"

"Whatever," he grumbled. "You tellin' this story, or am I?"

Landry continued. "So the incident in Asher occurred fifty years before you were born."

"Yep. I heard about it as a kid from Paw Paw — my grandpappy. He knew a lot. Sometimes I think he might have known a little too much, but the ones who went that night never admitted they was there. If he had been one of 'em, he woulda kept it quiet. Paw Paw told me lots of stories. If he wasn't there himself, he knew who was."

"Let's start at the beginning. I'd like to know about Asher. What did they do that made people mad enough to burn their town?"

"It goes way back. Asher's in the Bible: he was king of one of them lost tribes of Israel. The Sons of Jehovah cult thinks they're descended from him. Nobody knows where they came from, but they showed up in this parish before the War of Northern Aggression." He stopped and shot a grin at Ruby, who shook her head in mock disgust. "Depending on when they arrived, Abbeville and Perry might have already been here. But the cult folks didn't seem to want to socialize. They went downriver from civilization and built a town all to themselves."

The history lesson might end up being helpful, but Landry didn't have time to waste. "If the cult built Asher years before the men burned it in 1880, what did they do to make people so angry?"

"Paw Paw said they was real different, and they scared folks in Perry and Abbeville. In the days before the fire, two of 'em would come to town for supplies every so often. Looked like Abraham Lincoln, with their beards and stovepipe hats and black suits. One guy would stay in the boat while the other marched through town like he was a king or somethin'. He'd go from store to store and buy supplies.

"Once a month on a Saturday they'd set up tables in Magdalen Square and sell stuff they made — furniture, quilts, jelly and things like that. Only the men came, never the women, and they only spoke what they had to. Just did their business and went back home. People bought from them 'cause the stuff was good quality, but then they'd go home and talk about the strange-looking men. Because they was so different, it made the people skittish."

"Being different's one thing," Landry said, "but is that enough to burn the town and kill people?"

Lee jerked his head up and looked in Landry's face with a scowl. "Now wait just a minute, young feller. Nobody said nothin' about no killin', and nobody's ever proved it. My granddaddy wouldn't have been part of somethin' like that. He wasn't even there that night. He couldn't have known about a killin'."

Landry had hit a nerve when he brought up the murders. The old man was hiding something. "I'm sorry. I shouldn't have said that. So the vigilantes burned Asher because the people were different?"

"That, and them girls disappearin'. That was really what done it."

This was interesting. "What girls? When did they disappear?"

"Every now and then. People blamed the rougarou at first, but smart folks say there ain't no such thing. My pa swore they was real, so I grew up believing too. Parents would scare their kids into behavin', know what I mean? 'If you don't quit sassin' your momma, the rougarou's gonna come snatch you away.' Stuff like that."

He paused and turned to Ruby. "Are you gonna give me that cigarette now, or am I gonna have to get it myself?"

"All right, Mr. Lee." She exhaled an extended, theatrical sigh and handed him a pack of Winstons. He shook one out, tapped it on the filter end a few times, and lit it. As he did, Landry observed how steady his hand was. For ninety-seven, this old fellow was doing okay.

Ruby said it was getting close to lunchtime and Landry needed to wrap things up soon. "He takes a nap in the afternoons, and then I drive him over to the community center so he can socialize."

He coughed hard and asked Landry where he came from.

"The next parish over. I grew up in Jeanerette."

"Iberia Parish. I'll be damned! I knew you was a coonass too! You surely heard stories about the rougarou when you was little, right?"

"Yes," Landry replied, surprised at how often the rougarou came up in conversation around here. "Can you tell me more about the girls who disappeared?"

"My grandpa said it started way back in the 1800s. They was teenagers, snatched just as they was blossoming, if you get my drift. People spread rumors that the girls were being used in some kind of ritual sacrifice."

A ritual sacrifice? Could the cult have been far more hellish than just a commune of like believers?

"Did the disappearances stop after the town burned?"

"No, but the kidnappings got real regular. Seemed like they happened about every ten years. I remember some of them — they really upset the families, as you might imagine. The cult was easy to blame because they was so different, but after the fire, they disappeared. People still said it was them, and whoever was sheriff at the time would investigate, but accordin' to my grandpa, nothin' ever turned up. A whole bunch of teenagers went missing through the years. It was sad, but then what was sadder was the girls they did find. That got everybody's hackles up — what he done to 'em and all that."

Did I hear him correctly? "You mean they found some of the kidnapped girls?"

"Yeah, three of 'em turned up dead down by the river near Asher. I was a kid when they found the first one. I'll never forget it 'cause it scared the hell out of everybody for weeks. Nobody ever locked their doors at night before then, but from then on they damn sure did. What Billy — I mean, what the killer done to her made people's skin crawl."

"Billy? Billy Whistler did it? What happened?"

"I didn't say nothin' about Billy Whistler. Don't put words in my mouth. What he done was gouge out her eyes. Maybe even before she was dead, some said. That scared the bejeezus out of people, me included."

Landry wanted to know more about Billy Whistler later. Right now he guided Lee to stay on track. "You said they found three girls, and you told me about one of them. What about the other two?"

"They was like the first. Somebody found the bodies at Asher. The latest one was maybe twenty years ago, and there was another one back in the forties or fifties. I got home from the Army in 1947, and seems like it was a few years later that she got killed. It was the same thing every time. The very same thing happened to each one of them, and it made everybody nervous as hell, 'cause they figured the same guy done it. But he couldn't have, could he? They was years and years apart, those killings. The murderer woulda been an old fart like me by the time he killed the last one."

Ruby looked at her watch. "My, the time's flown by. We have to go inside now." She stood and straightened her skirt.

"One second," Landry insisted. "You said the same thing happened to those girls. Are you talking about their eyes being gouged out?"

Ruby maintained her smile, but now she was firm. "We're done now, Mr. Landry. He's had enough for today, and this kind of talk doesn't help his blood pressure. I'm going in to fix his lunch now."

Landry stood and shook the old man's hand. "You've been very helpful, but I'm sorry we didn't get around to Billy Whistler. Do you mind if I come back?"

"Son, you come back anytime you want. I'd a lot rather be talkin' to you than those old farts over at the center. Bring me a carton of Winstons when you come, and don't give 'em to the old battle-ax here," he added with a wink as he pointed to Ruby.

She gave Landry her cell number, saying it would be best to wait a couple of weeks before coming back. Long visits like the one today took a toll on Lee. He'd probably nap all afternoon.

Landry walked with them as she pushed his wheelchair. When they got to the porch, Lee stopped Ruby and turned to Landry. "Them other two girls had their eyes gouged out too. That's what I meant when I said 'same thing.' See you next time."

As he drove back to New Orleans, Landry couldn't get the girls out of his mind. According to Lee, girls had disappeared from time to time for over a hundred years. Only three of them were ever found, and each of those was gruesomely mutilated in the same manner.

If most of the girls disappeared, why were three bodies found? What was different about them? Had they escaped somehow, only to die in the same place, along the banks of the river near Asher?

The cult vanished after the fire, but some people believed they were behind the murders, one of which happened twenty years or so ago, according to Lee. How could that be? Were the Sons of Jehovah still close by, watching and waiting to trap helpless teenagers? Were they bloodthirsty murderers who gouged out their victims' eyes?

Before he met Lee Alard, Landry's trip to Abbeville had been interesting, but the old man's story was downright incredible. A sense of anticipation and excitement began to creep over him, the way it always did when he realized there was a mystery that lay in front of him.

A tragedy had happened at Asher a long time ago, and some residents of this parish thought it never ended. There was a lot more work to do here, and he was eager to get started.

CHAPTER SIX

Back at his office, Landry searched the web, visited the history museum at the Cabildo on Jackson Square, and examined nineteenth-century documents from Vermilion Parish. He copied everything he found, and soon his desk was overflowing with articles and information on the parish, the Sons of Jehovah, the legend of Billy Whistler, and Asher itself.

As he cross-indexed his findings in an Excel spreadsheet, something surprised him — not what he found, but what he didn't.

Vermilion was a quiet parish. The kidnappings and murders of three teenaged girls would have been an explosive story. He should have come across banner headlines in papers as far away as Lafayette and Baton Rouge. But it was just the opposite.

The first body was found in 1930. It merited only one sterile, sad second-page paragraph in the Abbeville paper. An unnamed seventeen-year-old female disappeared from her home in town, and someone discovered her body the next morning. Lee said she was found in Asher, but the article vaguely described the site as "along the river south of town." The poor child's name wasn't even mentioned, Landry reflected. What a tragic event for her family, and what a dismissive paragraph to sum up a life and death.

There was a little more substance to the news article on the 1950 murder. Someone had abducted a fifteen-year-old girl after a church social in Abbeville. Late that night two fishermen saw a body lying on the shore "near the ruined town of Asher." Since she was a minor child, her parents asked that her name not be printed.

The third girl died in 2000. Seventeen-year-old Mollie Manning was the daughter of a prominent local businessman. A three-paragraph front-page article reported that a man running crawfish traps in the middle of the night heard a commotion along the Vermilion River somewhere south of Perry. He pulled to the bank and found Mollie's still-warm body. He told authorities he thought he'd "run someone off," but the killer got away.

Her obituary appeared two days later. It was bland and factual and said nothing about the circumstances of her death. A one-liner at the bottom read "Hebert Funeral Home, trusted by families since 1875." Landry went to the Hebert website and saw that it was the oldest of the parish's several funeral parlors and handled more services than the others combined. That was good information — he'd visit the place next time he was in Abbeville.

The next month was hectic, and after weeks away, Landry was eager to return to Vermilion Parish. He called Ruby and learned that Lee was just out of the hospital after suffering a serious respiratory infection. At his age, recovery would be a slow process, and he was on a breathing machine, making conversation impossible. Ruby promised to keep in touch.

Disappointed that he wouldn't hear more of Lee's fascinating stories, Landry decided to make the trip anyway. There were other things to investigate. He called Darlene and made a reservation at Caldwell House again.

He requested an upstairs bedroom just to see if anything would be different during the night. She said this time he'd have company, a couple from Texas in town planning a wedding. Their room would be just across the hall from his own.

He got to town around ten and went straight to the courthouse. Grace's face beamed when he asked if they could talk privately. She nodded conspiratorially, tossed a huge smile over her shoulder to her coworkers, took him out into the hall, and led him to a door marked "Jury Room."

"We don't have a lot of trials, so this room's always empty," she said as they sat at a long wooden table. "I can hardly wait to hear what brought you back!" Her face positively beamed with excitement.

This time he was seeking information on three girls who were murdered at Asher. He showed her the newspaper articles about the teenagers. He knew the years of death but only one name — Mollie Manning.

"I remember her death like it was yesterday," Grace said, recalling that every mother barricaded the doors at night for months after that incident. "I even went out and bought a gun," she admitted.

The other deaths occurred before Grace was born, and she hadn't heard about them. Landry pointed out the similarities — each was a teenager who'd been abducted in town and dumped at Asher.

"You know more than I do, and I was born and raised here! Who on earth told you all that?"

"An old fellow in Perry. He knows a lot of history, much of it passed down from his grandfather. Lee Alard's his name."

"Oh yes, Mr. Lee! He's a great guy, full of spunk too, always has been. Whoever put you onto him did you a favor. He's lived here all his life, and he knows this parish better than anybody!"

Landry quickly learned his job was going to be simpler this time. Parish birth and death records back to 1910 had been entered into a database, and that meant no bulky ledgers full of semi-legible handwritten entries to comb through.

She put Landry in front of an old PC and pulled the death records for 1930. There were hundreds of entries. Without a name, date of death or cause, Landry was stymied.

Thinking of how to narrow the search, he glanced at a group of entries and found a single word that might help. Hundreds of people might have died in the parish that year, but he bet not that many were murdered.

He sorted the data by cause of death and entered the word *homicide*.

That narrowed the field to a manageable thirty-seven names. He eliminated the men and the females older than twenty, and one name remained. Mary Tallant of Abbeville, age seventeen, died on May 26, 1930, at an unspecified location in Vermilion Parish. The cause of death was homicide — multiple injuries to face. He found that choice of words odd.

He turned to the 1950 murder and performed the same search. Fifteen-year-old Carole Nichols was from Abbeville. She died "in the parish" on May 26. The cause of death was homicide — fatal wounds.

Now he knew her name and date, but nothing else. And like the first, the words used to describe the cause of death raised questions.

Mollie Manning's death certificate provided the most information. She was seventeen at the time of her death on May 26, 2000, "near Asher." She was the only one whose body had been autopsied. That report would have been helpful to review, but he knew that would be impossible. HIPAA regulations made things like autopsy reports off-limits.

Grace printed a copy of the three records and Landry compared them. One interesting communality was that a single funeral home — Hebert in Abbeville — handled arrangements for all three.

He reviewed his notes and saw he'd neglected to write Mollie's cause of death. Already knowing which box had been ticked, he looked at the certificate.

Homicide, just like the others. But the next chilling words revealed much more.

Eyeballs forcibly removed.

The harsh words made him gasp. Lee Alard had told him the girls had their eyes gouged out, and that part of his story was true.

"Are you all right?"

"I'm fine. It's just … I've just figured something out. It took some gruesome words, but things are coming together."

She looked at the death record but didn't immediately notice. He pointed and she raised her hands to her face.

"Oh my! The poor child! I'd forgotten that happened to her. What kind of monster —"

Landry wasn't listening. He was comparing the death certificates, looking again and again to be sure he was right about what he was seeing. Everything was starting to make sense now.

The girls died on the same day — the twenty-sixth of May. Lee said many other girls disappeared over the years, and Landry would have bet the farm that they vanished that day too.

That day held special significance for the Sons of Jehovah cult, because on May 26, 1880, men from Abbeville burned their town.

CHAPTER SEVEN

Landry wanted to put this puzzle together. There was a lot missing, but several pieces just fell into place, and he realized the girl who left the message was probably telling the truth. He had more stops to make, and as successful as this trip had been already, he might learn even more.

The sheriff's office was a one-story building across the street from the courthouse. He walked in and asked for Sheriff Conreco. The girl at the front counter turned to the back of the room. A large man in his fifties sat behind a desk in a small office. When he glanced up, the girl motioned to him.

"What can I do for you?" the sheriff asked. The buttons on his uniform shirt struggled to contain his girth, and the armpits were stained.

"I'm Landry Drake. I'd like to talk to you about the disappearances in Asher."

"Landry Drake?" the girl gasped. "*The* Landry Drake?"

Conreco shot her a stern look. "Planning a show up here, son?"

"Too early to say. I'm just gathering information right now. May I talk with you for a moment in your office?"

"We can talk right here."

The office wasn't busy; a few deputies and some clerks worked at their desks, but there were no visitors other than Landry, and no one was watching him. He lowered his voice and said, "A lot of girls have disappeared since 1880. It may have something to do with the night they burned Asher."

The sheriff raised his eyebrows just enough that Landry noticed. He continued. "They found bodies at Asher in 1930, 1950 and 2000. Were you on the force when they found Mollie Manning's body twenty years ago, Sheriff?"

Conreco nodded, his face impassive. He turned and spit tobacco in a nearby trash can.

"Fishermen found Mollie Manning's body on the riverbank. She had her eyes gouged out."

"Where the hell did you hear that?"

"I saw her death certificate at the courthouse, and I read an article about it. It seemed brief for such a sensational crime. This had to be the biggest thing in Vermilion Parish in years — a girl from a prominent family kidnapped and murdered. The story didn't talk about the investigation. Were the state police called in?"

"I don't recall. Wouldn't have been a case for them, regardless. Local thing, happened right here in the parish. Nothing we couldn't handle."

"What was your take on the mutilation?"

The sheriff looked away. "Boy, it's been twenty years. Lot of time's passed. I don't recall exactly. Don't you worry about twenty-year-old murders. There's nothing about them that a big-shot TV investigator would care about."

Landry watched Conreco's eyes dart around the room as he spoke. *He's lying.* "Would you mind if I looked at the file on her case?"

"It's an open case. Reporters don't just stroll in here and look at open cases."

"Do her parents still live around here?"

The sheriff seemed to have had enough. He pulled his pants up by the belt loops, leaned on the counter, and said, "You listen to me, Mr. Drake. The girl's murder is an open case, like I told you. If you stick your nose in other people's business — especially *my* business — you're going to find yourself on the receiving end of an obstruction of justice charge. There wasn't anything about that case that deserves a *celebrity* like you coming to our town and stirring everything up. Vermilion's a nice quiet parish, and people like it that way. They don't want people's dirty laundry plastered all over the television."

"So there *is* dirty laundry?" Landry interjected. That turned out to be the last straw.

"I've tried to be nice to you, mister big-city reporter. You're going places you don't want to go. You got no business in Asher. I don't want to see you again in this parish. Consider yourself warned. If I catch you sneaking around, I'll slap you so far behind bars it'll take your lawyer a week to find you."

On what charge? Landry considered pushing his luck, but he chose discretion. "You've been very helpful, Sheriff. Thank you for your time." He left the building, went to Dupuy's and had a crawfish platter. Instead of eating at the bar, Landry took a table so he could put his thoughts together. He wondered if the sheriff was serious about that "get out of town" talk. Landry had paid for a room tonight and he had at least one more stop to make. He was already here, so he'd finish what he came for.

The Hebert Funeral Home was just down the street. It reminded Landry of a church; everybody spoke in low voices, hidden speakers filled the rooms with soft organ music, and the furniture made it feel like a grandmother's parlor.

Landry learned that David Hebert IV, the owner, was out at the moment. An associate escorted Landry into a small room, closed the door, and pointed to an overstuffed chair next to an end table where a box of Kleenex sat. The man took an identical chair opposite him. He introduced himself and asked Landry's name. He didn't appear to recognize it, which Landry thought was a good thing, given the reason he was here.

"Thank you for coming to Hebert's, Mr. Drake. How may we be of service?" the fellow asked in the gentlest voice Landry had ever heard from a man.

Landry had several deaths to check out, but he decided not to reveal everything at first. He would start with the 1880 cult murders and then bring up the three girls.

"I'm looking for information. I read online that this is the oldest funeral home in Abbeville, dating back to 1875. Nowadays you conduct more services than the other establishments in town combined."

"Yes, sir, that's correct. We're proud of our history; generations of families have put their trust in Hebert's. We're prepared to handle every need, which means less stress and worry for you and the family during a time of grief and sorrow. May I ask who is the deceased?"

"I'm not here about that. I'm researching some deaths that happened a long time ago, and I was hoping you could help me get information about them."

The man's brow furrowed slightly. "I doubt it, sir. We pride ourselves on the privacy of our clients."

Unsure if the information was true, Landry assured him what he wanted to know was public information. "Seven men died in 1880. I can't find out anything about them."

"My, that was a long time ago. I'll see what I can do. May I have their names?"

"That's the problem. I don't have their names. But I know they all died on the same night, May 26, 1880, in a town called Asher."

"Asher? I haven't heard of it. Is it in this parish?"

"Yes. It's a ghost town today. Are you from around here?"

"No. I'm from Missouri. Mr. Hebert was looking for an associate and I ended up here in Abbeville."

"If you were born in this parish, you might have heard of it. Asher was on the river around ten miles south of here. The town burned in a fire that night when the people died."

"Oh, I see. They died in a fire."

Not exactly, Landry thought, but he didn't correct the man.

He continued. "I'd think your best bet is to search the courthouse records. Anyone who died in the parish would be recorded there."

Landry said he'd tried there but wasn't successful. He didn't reveal these were cult members who kept their information to themselves.

"Let me see what I can find out," the man offered. "If Hebert's didn't handle the arrangements, then there may be nothing in our files. But seven people on the same day, all from one little town — that's beyond coincidental. So long as one of them is your relative, I think I can let you know what I find. Is that true?"

Landry nodded. There was nothing wrong with a little subterfuge to get information that should be public anyway.

He checked messages on his phone while he waited. Ten minutes later, the door opened and a tall, gray-haired man in his sixties, impeccably dressed in a dark pinstripe suit and maroon tie, stepped into the room.

His face was stern and his jaw set. "I'm David Hebert, Mr. Drake. I understand you inquired about some deaths, one of which was your relative. If that's true, why don't you know the name of the deceased?"

Landry stood and extended his hand, but the funeral director refused to shake it. "I wasn't asking for private information," he began, but Hebert interrupted him.

"This discussion is over, Mr. Drake. My establishment will not be party to the sensationalism you stir up everywhere you go. The problems down in Asher ended more than a century ago, and I doubt anybody in Vermilion Parish wants them aired again. You'll get no help from me, and I'd suggest lying to get information isn't how a professional reporter should go about it."

"I asked for you first, and I wasn't trying to hide anything," Landry protested, but the man took his arm and steered him to the front door.

"Here's some free advice," Hebert said as he deposited Landry on the porch. "Forget you ever heard of Asher. The founding families of this town have long memories. If you open some doors, there's no way to close them again. Poke around enough and you'll find yourself in grave danger. Better safe than —" He paused.

"Than what, Mr. Hebert? Better safe than sorry?"

"That's not the word. I've watched a few of your so-called documentaries. It's nothing but sensationalism designed to give uneducated people the heebie-jeebies. I understand that's what makes money for you people. But this is different. Asher's no haunted house story you tell around the campfire. It's no 'ghost standing on the widow's walk, waiting for her husband to come home.' Asher is real. It's evil — do you understand me? Pure evil. Better safe than *dead*. Get out of this parish and stay out. That's my advice to you."

"You talk like Asher still exists. It's been gone since 1880. You must be joking."

"I never joke, Mr. Drake. Stay away from Asher. The buildings may be gone, but that's far from the end of that story. The Sons of Jehovah —" He caught himself, turned, walked through the front door, and closed it behind him.

Landry walked to his car, far more intrigued than when he arrived this morning. Most times when someone demanded he back off a story, there was something to hide.

That was what appeared to be happening here, and everywhere he turned, someone new was in the middle of it.

Asher is still evil today? The buildings are gone, but that's not the end of the story? And what was he going to say about the Sons of Jehovah?

When he set up this trip, Landry had thought about going down to Asher. Now it was an imperative. Other than his friend Grace, everybody he met was hell-bent on getting him out of this parish. Maybe if he saw Asher for himself, he'd learn more about why.

———

David Hebert closed the door to his office, picked up the receiver, and dialed a number he'd committed to memory over twenty years ago.

A man answered on the first ring. "What do you want?"

The man's condescending tone always rankled him. "What do you think, Joel? I'm calling this number, and therefore we have a problem. Assemble the others."

CHAPTER EIGHT

The things that happened today puzzled Landry. He couldn't believe Sheriff Conreco would lock him up just for spending the night in Abbeville. In the twenty-first century there were rules. Sometimes though, rules didn't matter. Although he lived in the city, he'd grown up a rural boy, and he understood that things were different out here. He had to stay out of the sheriff's way and obey the law so there would be no grounds for detaining him. But just in case, he sent his boss an email explaining the sheriff's threat and what he was doing for the rest of the day.

Several hours of daylight remained — enough to go ten miles downriver if he could find a ride. He had to visit Asher.

Last time when he'd crossed the drawbridge into Perry, he'd seen a few ramshackle buildings and some boats tied to a dock. A sign along the road offered fishing-guide services, and today he turned onto a dirt road that led to the river.

The place seemed deserted. The first shack he came to had an old metal sign: "Catfish Guidry — Fishing and Swamp Tours." Inside sat an unshaven man in his forties wearing a faded, torn T-shirt that read *Mardi Gras 2004*. He had his feet propped up on an old table, and he held a dog-eared copy of *Field and Stream* while nursing a beer. Landry glanced at his watch, thinking it was a little early for drinking, although he'd done it himself.

The man noticed his move. He closed the magazine, put it on the table, and drawled, "You late for an appointment? Or were you seein' if I was open so you could buy yourself a beer? Or were you just being judgmental about people who think it's five o'clock somewhere?" He broke out into a grin that showed he was playing around.

Landry laughed. "Apologies. None of my business. I'm looking for someone to take me down the river. I saw the sign. Are you Catfish?"

"That's me. Fishing? Sightseeing? Shootin' gators? Whatcha looking for?"

"None of the above. I want to go to Asher."

"Asher? What the hell for? Damn place burned down. Ain't nothin' left of it."

Not according to David Hebert.

"I'm doing some research. I want to poke around the ruins. How far is it?"

"Maybe twenty minutes away. You a writer?"

He doesn't know who I am. It was refreshing to be anonymous. "I'm not a writer. I work for a TV station in New Orleans."

"TV, huh? I ain't watched TV since my set went out what — two years ago? Maybe longer. Hard to quit, but you don't miss it once it ain't squawking at ya all day long. Know what I mean?"

Landry paid Catfish a hundred dollars for the round trip to Asher. They climbed into an ancient wooden jon boat, Catfish loaded a cooler, and then he fired up an Evinrude outboard motor that looked even older than the boat. It died once and then again, but at last it caught. Landry wondered if the boat would stay afloat for twenty minutes, and he was both glad and surprised to find a life vest stowed under his bench. As they pulled away from the dock, Catfish told him to grab a couple of brews.

He took two Dixie longnecks from the cooler and passed one down. He took a slow draw while Catfish drank his in one long gulp and asked Landry for another. They headed south on the river, with the motor sputtering and coughing every few minutes as though the end of its life was near.

As they meandered down the beautiful countryside, Catfish talked about local politics, the best places for dinner in Abbeville, where to pick up what he called loose women, and how much nicer it was to live in Vermilion Parish than Orleans.

Catfish had an opinion for every subject. "Nawlins is nothin' but drunk tourists," he declared. "It's sleazy, and the Mafia owns everything."

Landry objected, saying every town had its drawbacks. "You're saying New Orleans is nothing more than Bourbon Street, and that's not fair. That's one tiny part of the city. That's not the real New Orleans. How about the rest of the French Quarter? It has culture, world-class cuisine, excellent music and entertainment. You can have all that without ever running into drunk tourists, sleazy bars or the mob."

The guide shrugged, took out an unfiltered cigarette, and lit up. Landry glanced at a five-gallon gas can sitting an inch from Catfish's leg, but the man didn't seem concerned.

"Toss me another beer, will ya?" Landry handed it over; Catfish drank some and settled back.

"Is Catfish your real name?"

The guide laughed so hard he spit beer halfway across the boat. "My momma was a coonass for sure, but even she wasn't redneck enough to name her kid Catfish. My given name's Laurence, but I've been Catfish since I was in first grade. It suits me just fine."

Landry agreed it fit him better than Laurence, and he switched the subject to Asher. "What do you know about it?"

"What's there to know? They burned it down a long time ago."

Landry wanted to hear Catfish's version. "Who?"

"Accordin' to my grandpa, who heard it from his daddy, it was some men from Abbeville, back in the eighteen hundreds. They come down one night in boats and torched everything. It was a decent-size town, I guess, but after their little visit there wasn't nothin' left."

"Why would they do that?"

"'Cause Asher was some kind of cult town. The people called themselves the Sons of Jehovah. Somethin' out of the Bible, grandpa said. They was like the Amish on steroids — they didn't allow anything modern, their women never went to town, and there was Bible-thumpin' and preachin' all night long sometimes. People on the river could hear them yellin' and stuff.

"Now and then the men would come to Abbeville for supplies. They scared folks with their long beards, strange old-fashioned clothes and such. I guess some men in Abbeville just had enough. They went down there to see for themselves what was goin' on, they didn't like what they found, and they burned the place to the ground."

"Were they arrested?"

"Nope. Nobody to arrest, because nobody ever told who went. It's a secret that lasts even now. Rumors went around as to who was there, but no one admitted anything. People in town didn't really care; they was just glad that bunch was gone."

Landry wondered if Catfish's relative had been one of those who went to Asher. "So the cult disbanded after that?"

"Nobody knows. Some say that was the end of 'em, and they broke up and went every which way — north, south, east and west. Others say they went deep into the bayou and built themselves another town. Those folks say they're still out there today, hiding in the swamp somewhere. Some people think that's how the stories about Billy Whistler got started. Ever hear of him?"

Landry perked up. He'd kept quiet about Billy Whistler because he didn't want Catfish to know the legend was the main reason Landry was sitting in a leaky old boat heading down the Vermilion River to a ghost town. Now that Catfish had mentioned him, Landry jumped in.

"Tell me about him."

"It has to wait until the trip back. We're here." He eased the boat to shore, hopped out, and pulled the bow up on dry land. They came to a chicken-wire fence stretched across the shoreline, and Catfish used his all-purpose knife to cut a hole big enough for them to crawl through.

While they were poking around the ruins of Asher, Catfish cocked his head. "Listen! Hear that warbling sound? That's Billy Whistler!"

"I didn't hear anything." They listened, but it didn't happen again.

At that point Landry sent Catfish back, saying he wanted to check a few things out on his own. Catfish sat in the boat, thinking that coming here was a waste of time, but it wasn't his call. If this guy wanted to pay him a hundred bucks for a ride to a ghost town, that was fine with him.

After a while Landry returned and they cast off. It was a beautiful late afternoon as they headed back north toward Perry, and Catfish said he was getting hungry.

"You eaten at Cajun Claws yet?" he asked, and Landry said he hadn't. "Best damn crawfish in the world. Like little lobsters they're so big. People come from all over to eat there. It ain't no fancy French Quarter place like you're probably used to, but their food is the best. One piece of advice — don't go in there wearin' a nice white shirt. You'll end up a mess when you dig into all them mud bugs."

"Can you tell me about Billy Whistler now?" Landry asked, changing the subject while keeping Cajun Claws in mind for dinner. Catfish's description of those crawfish had made his stomach rumble.

"I guess you'd better hand me another longneck, brother. I'll tell you a tale that used to scare the shit out of me. You can't make this stuff up, know what I mean?"

CHAPTER NINE

Before he began, Landry asked if Catfish had gotten this tale from his grandfather too.

"Not exactly. I mean, he may have told me, but kids grew up hearing this story. People in this parish have talked about Billy Whistler for — hell, I don't know — way over a hundred years. His story's all mixed up with the cult's."

A bad thing happened that night, he continued, even worse than the town's destruction.

"You mean the murders?"

"Murders? What makes you think there was murders?"

"I saw an old article that said some cult members died that night. Have you heard that?"

"Maybe. Everything's just rumors and whispers. People don't talk about it, like I said earlier. Some said there was a hangin', but to this day nobody knows for sure. Except them men that went down there, I guess, but they're long since dead and gone."

"They hanged one of the cult members?"

"No, people say it was one of the men who came down from Abbeville. The townspeople caught him and hanged him in a tree. But that's just a rumor, like I said." He paused. "I shouldn't have told you that. Don't go around town saying Catfish said something about a lynching. I got enough problems already."

"Don't worry; I'll keep quiet. So, the vigilantes didn't murder anybody that night?"

"Boy, you sure ask a lot of questions. Why don't you read some more of them old articles instead of prying everything out of me? You're gonna get me in trouble."

"What are you talking about? How could you get in trouble for something that happened ages ago? So you told me about a lynching in 1880. That was a bad thing, but it's old news."

He fidgeted in his seat, took the last beer without offering it to Landry, and downed it in one long series of swallows. "Old news to you, but it still matters, trust me. You gotta promise you won't tell anybody what I said, okay?"

Why is he so nervous? "Okay. I just don't get it."

"You know how stories start out, then they get changed and people add stuff, and they get bigger and bigger and scarier and scarier? No way to know now what's truth and what isn't. Some say even worse things than a lynching happened that night." He shook his head as if to clear the cobwebs. "Why the hell did I say that? We started out talkin' about Billy Whistler and that's what we're gonna talk about."

"Hang on a second. What do people say happened that night?"

He pondered the empty beer bottle in his hand, and Landry knew the thing he wanted more than anything right now was another one.

"I shouldn't have told you any of that. Asher's gone. The cult could have burned it themselves, for all anybody knows. There's no proof that vigilantes went down there, or someone got killed, or hanged in a tree, or anything else. So I should keep my mouth shut like I was told."

Landry looked him in the eyes. "Like you were *told*? By whom? Who's keeping the secrets?"

Beginning to sweat, he picked up a dirty rag and wiped his brow. "Quit pushing, mister! 'Tween your million questions and the beer, I'm gettin' frazzled. Let it go. If you want to hear about Billy, I'll tell you. If you don't, we can just sit here 'til we get back to my dock. It ain't far anyways."

"I don't mean to pry. The story's fascinating and it just left me with a lot of questions. But I do want to hear about Billy Whistler."

"Okay. Nothin' wrong with telling you about him. Keep in mind it's just a story, somethin' people made up to scare little kids. No truth to it."

This guy's trying hard to convince me these stories aren't true.

He explained that Billy Whistler had been depicted in many ways over the years. Sometimes he was an apelike creature, or a werewolf, or a ghoul who roamed the earth killing humans. He might have been around before 1880, but the sightings and the fanciful stories about him heated up afterwards. Catfish figured the Sons of Jehovah used an existing legend to make people afraid of them. They incorporated the horrible things the deformed monster did into their own stories. If outsiders thought the cult had power over Billy Whistler, they'd stay away from them.

Landry pushed a little harder. "Have you heard about girls from Abbeville disappearing over the years? I heard they found three. Some people say Billy Whistler did that."

The guide pulled the boat up to his dock. "Okay, mister. What's this all about? What were you doing down at Asher? You've been nosin' around town, haven't you? You was full of questions with me, but you know a lot more. I ain't talkin' about no girls, and I ain't talkin' any more about anything else. It's been a pleasure workin' with you, and I'm happy to take you again if you ever need me to. For now, let's call it a day."

Landry returned to the hotel, where he found Darlene and the Texas guests having a glass of wine in the parlor. He unpacked and joined them. She had revealed who their fellow lodger was, and over the next hour they peppered him with questions about his work and his shows. At last he begged off, saying he was meeting someone for dinner.

The dinner meeting was a white lie, but he was tired and ready for some good food and a beer or two. He drove to Cajun Claws and looked for Catfish, but the guide wasn't there. It was for the best; he had pushed the man hard, maybe too hard. The bar was noisy and packed solid, and he didn't want the conversation tonight anyway. He wanted time alone to process everything.

Caldwell House's dining room was abuzz with conversation when he came downstairs the next morning. The couple across the hall from Landry had awakened several times to the sound of bumps and scratches, but after his long day, Landry had slept straight through.

He helped himself to scrambled eggs, bacon, and French toast as Darlene told her new guests the same fascinating stories about the old house's history. At eight thirty he returned to New Orleans, his mind overflowing with questions about Catfish's tales and the belligerent attitudes of the sheriff and the undertaker.

CHAPTER TEN

A guard stepped out of a gatehouse and checked the sheriff's name off on a sheet on his clipboard. "Welcome to Baton Rouge. You're the first to arrive," he said as the massive iron gates swung open. "I think you know the way by now."

The sheriff drove along a paved driveway and around a corner, where a second guard directed him to a portico with massive Greek columns. Conreco had made this trip three times in the past twenty years. Every fourth time the Conclave met, this man hosted the group, and the ostentation always pissed Junior off.

A man in a dark suit opened his car door, welcomed him, took his keys, and drove away. *Who the hell has people park their cars for them?* It reminded him of the valet at Ruth's Chris in Lafayette, but that was a restaurant, not a man's home.

I don't care who he is, all this is too pompous for me. If I lived here, I wouldn't have all these lackeys running around. But deep inside he knew that was a lie. If he had money and power, he'd do it the same way. He'd want everyone to see that he could afford it and how important he was.

You never had to knock on the massive door; a man inside opened it just as you walked up. *Of course he did. We wouldn't want people to have to ring a doorbell, would we?* A butler escorted the sheriff to the back of the house and out onto the patio. It was a beautiful evening and the setting sun cast long shadows on dozens of beautifully manicured shrubs and trees.

I want this. It always happened, this sense of jealousy when he visited the homes of wealthy, powerful people. It would never be more than a dream. A lack of education, family connections and money stymied him. He could do nothing about it, but still it ate at him until he forced the thoughts away.

A waiter took his order for a Black Jack and Coke, and Junior sat by himself until the others arrived and their host joined them.

Once everyone had been served, the waiter left them. Now four men sat around a table, each of them between fifty and seventy years of age and from vastly different backgrounds. The sheriff knew them all. Two lived in his parish — the chairman, a timber magnate named Joel Morin, and David Hebert, a funeral director. He saw them now and then around town, but they weren't friends.

The fourth was Waymon Ferrara, in whose home they were meeting. Junior saw his face frequently on TV, but the only time they met face-to-face was at these meetings. The others wouldn't have given him the time of day if they weren't forced to. They came together for Conclave meetings and then they went their own ways. Rich, successful men didn't mingle socially with a sheriff.

The job of host was rotated, and every fourth time it was Junior's turn. He never invited them to his modest house because he was ashamed. Instead he rented the back room of the Elks Lodge in Abbeville. They all came and nobody said anything, but he believed they secretly mocked him for being poor.

These four men could not have been more dissimilar except for the one commonality that bound their lives together.

The secrets of the past.

As was the custom, a fifth chair sat at the foot of the table, honoring a comrade who died long ago. An empty chair, an unspoken reason, and before the meeting began, a toast to Auguste Dauphin, a brave, loyal soldier who gave his life for the cause. They stood and raised their glasses in a moment of silent tribute.

Joel Morin, their self-appointed chairman, called the group to order and said David Hebert had requested the meeting. He yielded the floor to the funeral director and took a seat as Hebert stood to address the group.

"I asked Joel to bring us together to discuss the sensationalist television personality Landry Drake." Hebert spent a few minutes on the background of the person his fans had nicknamed the "ghost hunter" and his television series called the *Bayou Hauntings*.

Waymon Ferrara couldn't believe his ears. "You brought us together to talk about a ghost hunter? I don't know about Joel, but my time's more valuable than that."

As soon as he heard Landry's name, Junior understood why they were here. He'd ordered Landry to leave town, but he wouldn't mention that right now. They might praise him for that move, or not. Better to see how things go. Sometimes the meetings turned nasty, and he didn't want to be on the receiving end of a load of shit.

The undertaker assured their host that the meeting was necessary. "Landry Drake came to my funeral home the day before yesterday. I was at my Kiwanis Club meeting, and I wouldn't be surprised if he timed his visit for when I might be out to lunch. He met with one of my young men, and I returned in time to put a stop to things. My associate promises me he gave the reporter nothing."

Morin tapped his fingers on the table. "Get to the point. Why did Drake come?"

"He wanted information about the seven Sons of Jehovah who died in Asher that night. He claimed one was a relative, even though he didn't have a name. That should have been clue enough, but in fairness, my young novice is new at this. He didn't know Landry Drake. Luckily I returned and took care of the matter."

Like their host, the chairman was irritated that Hebert had convened the Conclave over this. "And? And then what, David? Is there a point to all this?"

Intimidated, Hebert stumbled on his words and his hands began to shake. Junior kept his own hands folded in his lap, thankful he wasn't in the hot seat. He relished David getting his comeuppance. Maybe he wouldn't be so high and mighty now.

"Well, uh, that was it. I thought it important that we discuss this in person —"

Morin slammed his fist on the table. "How did you leave things with Mr. Drake, David? That's my question."

"Yes, sir, I apologize. I'm getting there. I gave the fellow a stern warning to stay away from Asher. I said it's an evil place. I told him the buildings were gone, but that's not the whole story. After the horrific picture I painted, I imagine he turned tail and drove back to New Orleans as fast as he could."

The chairman stared at him in disbelief. *Dear God, can the man really be this stupid? Two of our members are idiots. The sheriff doesn't have enough sense to know up from down, but at least he keeps his mouth shut most of the time. Hebert's another thing entirely; he's so pompous he's about to explode, and he hasn't the intelligence of an ass. But we four are linked by fate, and it is my unfortunate responsibility to shepherd the flock.*

"Sit down, David," he said calmly. He took a long drink and paused to gather his thoughts while the others waited in silence for Joel to castigate the undertaker. At last he stood, tented his fingers in front of him, and cleared his throat. He was a formidable man, accustomed to deference and a sense of reverence from other people because of his family's vast wealth and power. David shrank into his chair as Morin began to speak.

"On the surface you appear to be a capable man, a businessman who is a pillar of the community and a person to whom others look for guidance and advice. But in reality you *inherited* a respectable, profitable operation that any imbecile off the street could run, because your business requires nothing but dead bodies to be a success. You're neither a businessman nor an entrepreneur. You're a fourth-generation undertaker of average intelligence who had a gold mine dropped in his lap by your father. And him by his, I might add."

Keeping his eyes focused straight ahead, the sheriff forced himself not to smile.

Morin continued his tirade. "Your naivety never ceases to astound me. It seems at every Conclave you manage to prove yet again how little you know about dealing with people. Landry Drake's work is about searching for eerie supernatural things in the bayou parishes. You gave this man — who is an investigative reporter from a New Orleans television station — a stern warning to stay away from Asher. You told him it was an evil place, that there was more to the story than people knew, and in your own words, you painted a horrific picture." The chairman sighed. "Mr. Hebert, I must disagree with your assessment of Landry Drake's departure. After the tantalizing scenario you painted, I imagine going back to New Orleans was the furthest thing from his mind. You whetted the appetite of a hungry man. You tossed gasoline on a burning ember. You single-handedly stirred the passion in Landry Drake's soul.

If he didn't go straight to Asher after your revelation, he's not much of an investigator. Can you possibly comprehend what I'm saying?"

Beads of sweat formed on Junior's brow. *Damn, I'm glad I kept quiet. He'd have crucified me too.*

David cried, "That's not fair!"

"Shut up, you fool! You've done enough. Thank God you got one thing right. We did need to meet, because we have to control the damage you've done.

Morin turned to their host. "Waymon, I may need help later to diffuse this situation. For now, Sheriff, I want to know if Landry Drake visited Asher. If he did, go there yourself and find out what he was looking for. Get on this first thing in the morning and give me a report by the end of the day."

Junior raised his hand. "Sir, with all respect, how can I find out if he went there?"

The chairman barely maintained his composure. The stupidity of people was almost more than he could tolerate. He exhaled and spoke as if explaining the ABCs to a child. "Unless one walks through the bayou for miles, there's only one way to get to Asher, and that's by boat. How about checking with people along the river to learn if he rented a boat? That seems logical. I'm no sheriff, and it's obvious you don't process things as quickly as other people, but I've given you a good place to start. If you need any more guidance on how to do your job, you have my number."

Junior nodded and looked down again, wishing to God the Conclave wasn't part of his life. He hated these condescending asses and everything they stood for. He felt less of a man around them, and he hated that even more.

Joel Morin declared the meeting adjourned, and Ferrara asked whose turn it was to host next time.

"Mine," Morin said. "Next time we'll meet at my cottage on Vermilion Bay."

"Who knows how long that will be?" someone asked. "Our last meeting was two years ago."

"Mark my words, we will see each other soon, because our friend David here has ensured that we haven't heard the last of Landry Drake."

Waymon Ferrara, their host, stood at the door and bid each of them goodbye.

Joel shook Waymon's hand and said, "Good night, Governor. It's always good to see you, and thanks for hosting the Conclave. Frankly, David and Junior drive me insane."

Governor Ferrara slapped his friend's back and agreed. He walked Joel out, and they chatted with one of the governor's security staff until Morin's driver brought the car around.

CHAPTER ELEVEN

Sheriff Conreco turned on his light bar for the trip back to Abbeville and pushed the speed up to eighty. Tired from the ordeal, he wanted to get home.

The last thing he wanted was to go to Asher, and it was wrong to ask another Conclave member to do this. He could run into something that would compromise everything they stood for. He could send a deputy instead of putting himself at risk.

Joel Morin despised him. Junior felt it every time he opened his mouth. He'd get a roll of the eyes, a sneer and a condescending answer just like tonight. At least he wasn't the only one. David Hebert got his dressing-down too. Damn if the old man didn't castrate him right in front of everyone, and Junior had enjoyed every minute. Hebert had money, but nothing like Joel and Waymon had. Still, he acted uppity to everybody, and he got his tonight. Junior wished the chairman would get his too, but the super-rich never seemed to get what was coming to them.

Tomorrow he'd talk to the guides on the river. Landry Drake was a familiar figure; if he rented a boat, people would know. Junior hoped he hadn't. Maybe he had gone back to New Orleans like David told him to. It would make things a lot simpler, but it wouldn't be that easy. Landry was like a dog on a hunt; the undertaker put him on the scent and he was off and running.

It didn't take long to learn that the reporter actually did go to Asher. He might have known Catfish Guidry would be the one who took him. The sheriff knew Catfish, like everyone else in town. He'd been in the drunk tank more times than Junior could recall. How he made a living was anybody's guess, but he seemed fine with his situation. He lived in a back room of the shack that doubled as his office, and he had an old boat. Junior bet he was also debt-free. It didn't take many charters to buy longnecks by the case, probably his largest expense.

At first Catfish didn't know who the sheriff was asking about. He hadn't recognized Landry, but when Junior described him as a reporter from New Orleans, Catfish nodded.

Once Catfish confirmed he'd taken the reporter, it was easy to get his tongue loosened up. It didn't take much — one "get out of jail free" card did the trick. He had a pass the next time he ended up drunk and disorderly, and there would be a next time. There always was for guys like Catfish.

"What'd he do?" the guide asked, and Junior replied he was stirring up trouble in the parish. He took notes as Catfish described the trip downriver. He was pissed off that the reporter went straight to Asher after Junior ordered him to leave the parish. By God, he'd throw the son of a bitch in jail the next time he set foot up here.

"So we arrived," Catfish was saying as the sheriff tuned back in. "Have you gone there, Sheriff? There's a chain-link fence stretched across the shore about ten yards in from the bank. Looks like it's been there for years. It's got no trespassing signs hanging on it. Wasn't any big deal to get through, but it made me wonder who did it. Wonder who owns that land anyway?"

That was a good question, and Conreco made a mental note to find out. "What did you all do there?"

"All that's left is a bunch of foundations, and the underbrush was so thick it was hard to see them. I was there a long time ago, but I'd forgotten about them foundations. Lots of 'em. Must have been a helluva fire. Did you say you've been down there?"

Junior shook his head. He also didn't want to go there.

"Like I say, it looks like there was lots of houses and then near the river a long street that would have been for stores and whatnot. Those cult folks built themselves a proper town. Hundred and fifty people or more lived there, from the stories I've heard.

"All this talk's makin' me thirsty, Sheriff. Believe I'll have a beer. Want one?"

Conreco said no, and Catfish opened a Dixie longneck with a Pabst Blue Ribbon church key on a string nailed to his desk.

He keeps it within reach, Junior observed. *I'm sure it's well used.*

"What did Landry do?"

"He walked around and looked at stuff, as much as he could with the brush and all. He asked me what happened to the cult after the vigilantes came that night, and I told him nobody knows for sure. They killed seven of 'em, according to the stories, but nobody ever proved that either, I guess. He wanted to talk about it, though."

"It's a legend. You're right, nobody ever proved it. I hope you told him that."

"Yep. And hey, I just remembered something. I heard Billy Whistler!"

Junior looked up. "How much had you had to drink by then, Catfish?"

He laughed and belched, and a little beer dribbled down his chin. "Blame it on whatever you want, Sheriff. I heard him while we was standin' in the middle of Asher. Way off somewhere, almost like a whip-poor-will but different enough that I knew better. I heard it once before, when I was a kid."

"Billy Whistler's not real. It's a myth too; everybody knows that. What did Landry think it was?"

"He didn't hear it. I said, 'Listen, that's Billy Whistler.' Me and him cocked our ears, but nothing else happened. It came from back in the woods somewhere. Then he said with all these buildings there must have been a lot of people. Where did they all go? I told him the rumors. They moved somewhere way back in the bayous and set up another commune. Or they picked up and moved to Texas, or maybe Arkansas. Or they just broke up and went their separate ways."

"What other things did you tell him, Catfish? Did you tell him anything you shouldn't have?"

Honestly, after all that beer Catfish couldn't remember much of his conversation with Landry, but he knew how to keep himself out of trouble. "Hell no, I didn't. Some things ain't for outsiders. That pot don't need stirrin'. I kept my mouth shut like I been told."

"You sure?"

He nodded. "Why are you so worried anyway, Sheriff? You got a personal interest in this?"

"I'm the one asking the questions here. What else did you all talk about?"

"Before he sent me back to the boat, he asked where the graveyard was. He said every town has one. He asked where them seven they killed was buried. I said the story about killings wasn't true and I didn't know if they had a graveyard or not. That's when he told me to go back to the boat and wait."

Conreco looked up again. "You didn't go back, did you? Don't tell me you left him alone."

"Why not? It was his trip and he footed the bill. He walked off into the woods awhile, and then he came back. What's the big deal, Sheriff? What do you think he was looking for?"

Junior ignored him. "How long was he off by himself?"

"Thirty minutes or so; we was on the ground at Asher about an hour in all."

"Did he find the graveyard?"

"Beats me, but he told me there wasn't nothin' interesting to see."

"Then what did he do?"

"He tipped me fifty bucks and took my number. He told me he'd see me next time."

"Did he say when that would be?"

"Nope, but he was a friendly guy, and he tipped well. Personally, I hope he comes back soon."

So do I, the sheriff thought. *He and I will have a little talk if I catch him back in my parish.*

"Is there anything else you haven't told me?"

Catfish's memories were fuzzy. Had he told Landry about Billy Whistler and those missing girls from Abbeville? He didn't think so, and there damn sure wasn't any need to bring it up. All those questions made him tired, so he said no, there was nothing else he could think of.

"If he comes back, you call me, understand? This is important, and if I find out you took him back down the river without telling me, you're in deep shit."

Catfish gave a mock salute and said he would. For the rest of the morning he tried to think why the sheriff cared about that New Orleans guy and the trip downriver. And if he told that reporter anything he shouldn't have.

Junior couldn't avoid going. That damn reporter created all this mess, and Junior would pay him back for it. Joel Morin too — it wasn't safe for Junior to go there, and Joel knew it; it was like he was hoping something bad would happen.

My position in the Conclave is the same as his. Nobody outranks anybody else; we're all four equal. He can't tell me what to do. I'm the sheriff, and I'll decide who investigates what in this parish.

All that talk sounded great, but the chairman had issued an order. A long time ago, there had been five men joined by a common goal. But time and circumstances had changed everything. Today, decades later, there were four of them, not five. And Junior didn't have the backbone to stand up to Joel Morin.

He had to go to Asher, and it had to be now, because the chairman wanted a goddamn report by the end of the goddamn day.

CHAPTER TWELVE

The sheriff sat in the front of a Vermilion Parish Sheriff's Office boat with his young deputy at the tiller. They motored downstream, and Junior wished he had put in a few beers. Nervous, he took out his revolver and made sure it was loaded. When they arrived, he found the fence and no-trespassing signs Catfish had described, and they crawled through the hole he'd made.

"What is this place, Sheriff?" the young deputy asked, and Junior gave him a short version of the story. The place was abandoned, and the deputy asked what they were looking for.

"You ask too many questions, son. Come on. Do what I tell you and we'll be on our way back shortly."

He saw the foundations, and like Catfish, the size of the place surprised him. There were boot prints, possibly from Landry's visit, and he walked the town's perimeter, looking for trampled brush to indicate where Landry had gone into the woods. It wasn't hard to find.

Junior had brought this kid for one reason only, a reason no one would have suspected. He wanted someone else with him when he visited the graveyard. He might be the sheriff, but like most Cajuns, he had a healthy respect for the supernatural, and Catfish had said Billy Whistler was warbling in the distance. He always thought it was a legend, but what if it wasn't? No way was he doing this alone.

He shivered as he led the way down the path through dense foliage. He unhooked the strap on his holster again and rested his hand on his revolver. The deputy noticed and whispered, "Everything okay, Sheriff? Should I take my gun out?"

Damn, he didn't want to look like a coward. "Don't worry about it. I'm just being careful. You never know when you might come across a gator or a snake out here on the bayou."

They arrived at the graveyard, and Junior saw that someone was maintaining the area, keeping the grass trimmed and the brush and weeds cut back. Who was doing it and why? As far as he knew, no one lived within miles, and it was no longer being used.

This place spooked him. He felt a tingle in his spine as he tried to act nonchalant, walking around and brushing dirt off the flat stones that lay here and there. Some had carvings, but they were worn almost smooth. Two stones lay side by side at the head of two mounds of earth. He knelt and brushed away the dirt. That tingling sensation returned as he read the inscriptions.

JAMES SAVARY MARCH 2009
K SAVARY JAN 2007

This made no sense. Two people who had the same last name — relatives, maybe a husband and wife — buried just a decade ago.

This can't be right. It's a bizarre joke. The cult's long gone.

It came to him. He understood why the cemetery was well-maintained. The people who had supposedly abandoned Asher in the nineteenth century were nearby —

so close that they still used this graveyard for burials. His head spun with baffling questions. Two bodies lay in the ground right in front of him.

It was common knowledge that every cult member was either a Savary or a Lafont — and here were two from the recent past. His mind swam with memories, secrets too awful to reveal, and the realization that this wasn't over. It never ended and it spelled danger for him and the others.

They're here; I feel it. They know all about me. They know who I am.

I can feel their eyes on me. They're waiting, watching!

Junior's chest started to constrict; he sucked air in heavy gasps. He fell back hard on his butt and screamed, "Get me out of here! Get me away from them!"

Believing his boss was having a seizure, the deputy panicked. "Sheriff! Sheriff! What's wrong? You're too big for me to carry, sir! I'm calling for help!" He pulled out his walkie-talkie.

Junior shouted, "No!" The last thing he needed was more witnesses — the kid was bad enough. He had to pull himself together long enough to run to the boat. He was overweight and flabby, and it astonished the deputy when Junior leapt to his feet, ran to the path and disappeared into the woods. The younger man followed, trying to keep up with someone he would never imagine might outrun him.

As the deputy guided the boat away from shore, Junior touched his holster. His service revolver was missing. Frantic, he searched under his seat, behind him and on the floor of the boat.

"Have you lost something, sir?"

"Have you seen my pistol?"

"No, but remember you released the strap. It might have fallen out when you — uh, when you fell backwards at the cemetery. Should I turn around so we can go back and look for it?"

They should go back — he could send the kid to the cemetery to find it — but he was afraid to wait on the shore alone, even for a few minutes.

Pinpricks of pain shot through his chest. The poor deputy looked about to throw up, and Junior told him to go to Abbeville. "I'll take care of it later," he said, which surprised the deputy. The sheriff drilled into every new hire's head what happened if your service revolver went missing. You lost your job, period, no discussion. He was the sheriff though, and he could do whatever he wanted.

A figure waited in the bushes until the men left. When the sheriff fell, something hit the ground, but from where he hid, he didn't know what. He loped across the clearing to the graveyard, his hunched back causing his arms to dangle at his sides when he ran. He reached down and wrapped a filthy hand around the gun.

Although his brain didn't process information like other people's, it excited him to find something different. He wasn't sure what it was — he had seen guns before, but his long-term memory was faulty, and he didn't remember. He looked it over, stuck a long nasty fingernail into the barrel, and bit down on the grip to see how it tasted.

He touched every part of it, turning it over and over in his hands. The trigger had some play in it, and he pulled it back.

The boat was a mile away when the gunshot rang out through the woods.

Somebody had his weapon.

Someone was watching him.

I knew it! I felt it! Thank God I got away!

"Sheriff!" the deputy shouted, turning the tiller. "That was your gun! We should go back."

"Dammit, boy, mind your own business! You get us back to Abbeville as fast as you can. I'll take care of this later, like I already said."

"But, sir —"

"But sir nothing! If you breathe a word about this, you'll regret it. You understand?"

"Yes, sir," the confused kid replied. "I understand."

CHAPTER THIRTEEN

It was important to talk to Lee Alard again, and Landry called Ruby to see if he could visit.

"I'm sure he'd love it, but I'm not the one to ask anymore. Mr. Lee had to move out of his house, I'm sorry to say. It was a bad day when that happened, not only for him, but for me too. I'd kinda gotten used to that old coot, and I'm sure gonna miss him."

The last Landry had heard, Lee was at home after a long hospital stay for his bronchitis. That was only a few weeks ago, and he asked what had happened.

"He was just too weak. He wheezes with every breath now, and he has violent coughing fits sometimes. I'm not a nurse. I've been takin' care of folks for twenty years, but there comes a point when it's too much for me. Someone had to lift him in and out of bed, help him all night long, and things like that. He's got a nephew up in Opelousas who's his only relative. He picked up Mr. Lee and moved him into a nice nursing home there. I saw him the other day — he misses his independence, but he likes the place too.

He was playing dominoes when I was there. It's good for him to be around other people, don't you know?"

Landry took the name of the facility and said he enjoyed meeting her. Ruby asked for a heads-up if he did a show about their parish, and he promised he would call.

So Lee was in Opelousas. That was great news because when he went, he could ask Cate to join him. They had a friend named Callie Pilantro who owned Beau Rivage, a haunted plantation house on the Atchafalaya River just twenty miles from Opelousas. They'd been through an adventure with Callie at a spooky mansion called the Arbors. Joining forces to fight a malevolent spirit, the three of them had become friends, and Cate and Callie kept in touch. If they were in the area, spending the night at Beau Rivage was a must. Now he had to see if she was free to join him.

He called her office in Galveston. It had been two weeks since they'd been together, and he asked if she'd come for the weekend. Instead of meeting her in New Orleans as usual, he'd pick her up at the Lafayette airport and they'd spend two nights with Callie at Beau Rivage.

That sounded great to Cate, and she asked what was up in Lafayette. He explained he had an interview in Opelousas. He'd leave her at Beau Rivage, go see Lee, and come back to spend the rest of the weekend.

He told her about his trip to Abbeville and the curt warnings to stay out of the parish. "The sheriff and the undertaker invited me to leave immediately."

"Really? Usually it takes you longer than that to piss people off."

He laughed. "They're hiding something. The sheriff said he'd arrest me if I set foot in Vermilion Parish again. If I haven't done anything wrong, he would have no cause to detain me. That said, I wouldn't be surprised if he threw me in the pokey anyway when I go back."

"*When* you go back? You're already planning to disobey his order?"

"I have to. People are keeping secrets. It involves this ghost town south of Abbeville called Asher. I hired a guy with a boat and went down the river to find the ruins —"

She interrupted. "Wait a sec. Was that before the sheriff kicked you out, or after?"

"After."

"Are you serious? Two bigwigs, one of whom is the sheriff, tell you to leave, so you defy them instead?"

"It's a free country," he quipped. "Anyway, nothing happened. But the ghost town brings me to a question. It's a long shot, but does your dad own land there? It'd make it a lot easier for me to justify going if I had the owner's permission."

Cate's father Madison John "Doc" Adams had an unusual hobby. He bought tax liens and repossessed property for pennies on the dollar at auctions. He owned hundreds of parcels, most of them small and forgotten. Sometimes the previous owner paid the back taxes and redeemed his property. If he did, Dr. Adams made money. If he didn't, the land eventually reverted to Adams. He sold the land, often to an adjacent landowner, and he almost always made a decent profit.

She reminded him how much trouble they'd gotten into at the Asylum, an abandoned prison in Iberia Parish. Her dad owned the property, and they'd had a harrowing experience there. Landry turned the story into an episode called *Forgotten Men*.

"Remember how hard it used to be to keep up with what he owned? You had to rifle through stacks of paperwork all over the office. If you'd called me two months ago, I'd have started the process for you, griping all the way. I just finished entering every parcel of land into a database. I can cross-reference it every which way, and therefore it will be easy to pull up an answer for you. Hold on a sec."

She searched and said, "He has thirty-seven parcels in Vermilion Parish. Is it in a town, or is it rural?"

"It's an unincorporated town called Asher."

"I have no listings with Asher in the name. How about legal descriptions?"

"I'll check. I doubted your dad would own another property I'm interested in, but I thought I'd ask, since he's the biggest slumlord I know." That made her laugh. "A mob burned the town in 1880, and there's nothing left but foundations. I want to find out who owns it."

"Have you tried the courthouse?"

"I went there looking for something else, but I have a contact who's been helpful. I'll call her now and see what she can turn up. Send me your flight info and I'll pick you up Friday night!"

CHAPTER FOURTEEN

He asked Grace if she could find out who owned the land at Asher. She said she'd get right on it; it could take hours or a few days, and she'd call when she finished.

It made her happy he'd called on her again, and she asked if he minded her telling some friends. He agreed so long as she didn't mention exactly where his interests lay. For some reason, everything about Asher spelled trouble for him.

Grace told her coworkers, and word soon spread throughout the courthouse and across the street to the sheriff's office. A dispatcher named Sara told Junior that Grace was doing research for that TV investigator who came in last week. The sheriff cursed and stomped out of the office, slamming the door behind him and leaving the stunned clerk behind.

Junior stormed into the clerk's office wearing a scowl that frightened Grace. He demanded she tell him what Landry wanted, and she said that he was looking at land records.

"This is about Asher, isn't it? Dammit, I ordered that boy not to go down there. Tell me the truth, woman. He's got you looking up stuff about Asher, doesn't he?"

Grace had been born and raised a Southern Baptist. One thing she learned as a little girl was that if you start off lying, you'll make a mess of your life and go straight to Hell. As a result, she'd never been good at prevarication.

A tear trickled down her cheek. "I'm only trying to help him. What harm does it do? You know as well as I that there's nothing down there. It's a ghost town now. Why are you so dead set on keeping him out of Asher?"

Junior was livid. He had enough trouble with Joel Morin on his back, and now the damned reporter was sticking his nose into things that might get people in hot water.

"You want Abbeville splashed all over national TV by a sleazy ghost hunter? When he's finished with us, he'll have the world thinking Asher is spookier than Amityville. Tourists will descend on us like flies, looking for stuff that Landry Drake made up. I'll be damned if I'll let that happen. If you hear from him again, you call me first thing. And don't give him anything else. Understand?"

That Southern Baptist background also gave Grace a moral compass, a clear understanding of right and wrong. The sheriff had issues with Landry, but they had nothing to do with her. Land records were public information. Junior Conreco had no business berating her, and she wouldn't stand for it. She told him how she felt, and she refused to tell him anything about Landry.

"People have been spinning yarns about Asher for years," she continued. "Something bad happened down there, but people talk about it like it's some kind of mysterious thing. Everybody involved has been dead for ages. Who cares if my grandfather or yours was a vigilante? They acted like criminals, but it doesn't matter now. Here's how I feel. If there's something down there he shouldn't see, then tell me what it is. Otherwise, leave me be, and him too. He's a nice young man and he's doing nothing wrong."

He's a pain in the ass. Fuming, Junior forced himself not to lash out at Grace. She was right about the things she knew, but she didn't know the whole story. Only the Conclave did.

He took a deep breath, calmed down, and asked, "Who owns that property at Asher?"

"I haven't found out yet. Landry asked the same thing, and since the land records are public, I'll try to find out. When I learn the answer, I'll tell you both."

If he continued, she'd wonder even more what was behind all this, so he'd handle it another way. He went back to his office and called WCCY Television in New Orleans, told the receptionist his title, asked for the boss, and got Ted. Ted listened — there wasn't an opportunity to talk — and replaced the receiver after the sheriff hung up on him. Then the agitated manager walked down the hall to Landry's office.

"Do you have a minute?"

Landry looked up from his monitor and saw Ted standing in the doorway, his face as white as a sheet. "Hey, are you all right?"

"Better than you, I'd say. I just got a call from the sheriff over in Vermilion Parish."

Landry's laugh made things worse.

"What have you done over there to piss him off? He's the sheriff, Landry! There's a warrant for your arrest if you set foot in his parish again. He said to rein you in or the station might end up in trouble too."

"It's a bluff. Did he tell you what the charges were?"

"No, I got flustered and didn't ask. How can you smile? This is serious."

In the two days since Landry's return, he'd been working on other things. There was nothing to report about Asher yet, but now he brought his boss current.

"So what are you going to do next?"

"I'm going back. He can't arrest me — well, technically he can, but he can't hold me without cause. There's something going on. The more they try to keep me away, the more I'm convinced it's true. They're hiding something about Asher. It may involve some missing teenagers, or a mob that burned the town more than a hundred years ago, or something else entirely. But this is my job, and I know when I'm onto something. Don't worry; I'll be fine."

"You have no idea if you'll be fine. Why wouldn't I worry after all the close calls you've had? Everyone else here does the news or the weather or the sports, or talks about Mardi Gras or how many drunks are in the Quarter on weekends. Nobody who works for me ever gets in a jam, except one. You, however, are a different cat. You keep me awake at night. Because of you I buy antacids by the carton. Promise me one thing. Call our lawyers and tell them about the sheriff. Then someone can bail you out without calling me at two in the morning."

Landry apologized for giving Ted heartburn over the past couple of years, and he meant it. His boss was right — there had been one tight spot after another, but it was part of the job description. He promised to call the lawyers and to be on his best behavior in Vermilion Parish. His fingers were crossed on that last part. People up there got pissed off when he asked questions, so he must go and ask more.

Junior must have talked to Grace. That was how he found out Landry was still nosing around the parish. He called her and she whispered, "I'll call you right back. Too many listening ears around here."

He knew from her conspiratorial tone this was exciting to her, but he regretted involving her. If she ticked off the wrong people, she might lose her job.

He called the station's law firm and spoke to an attorney who'd helped with other situations. He agreed the sheriff was way out of bounds but cautioned that in some rural parishes, lawmen didn't always stay on the right side of the law. Sometimes outsiders ended up in big trouble before anyone knew there was a problem. He cautioned Landry to be careful.

A few minutes later Grace called back from a stall in the ladies' bathroom. She told him about the sheriff's visit and how he had scared her at first. "I had to tell him about Asher," she admitted. "I'm sorry, but there's nothing wrong with you seeing those records, and I told him so!"

"No need to apologize," Landry assured her. "I'm sorry I put you in the middle of all this."

"Now don't you say that! I love being involved! This is the most fun I've had in years! And I have news about who owns Asher. Hang on." He heard her unfold a piece of paper. "It's a company, not a person. The name is SOJ Land Company, and it owns two hundred acres along the river, including where Asher was. They got the property in a land grant in 1842."

SOJ. The Sons of Jehovah. "Interesting. Now I need to figure out who owns that company."

"I'm ahead of you on that! I called the Secretary of State in Baton Rouge to find out. There were two companies by that name, but one's too new. It started in 1967. It's the other one we want!"

Her resourcefulness impressed him, and he told her. "What did you find out?"

"Three men from Lafayette formed it in 1842. Micah Lafont, a lawyer; Caleb Lafont, a parson; and James Savary, a farrier. I'll bet the Lafonts were brothers."

"Great investigating! I'll acknowledge you if this ends up on TV. I'll even get you a seat to watch us tape it if you'd like to come. And I'm sorry about what happened."

That thrilled her, and she pooh-poohed his apology. "That sheriff won't scare me next time. I'm ready for him. He'd better watch out who he messes with!"

Landry thought, *It won't be you he messes with next time.   It'll   be   me.*

CHAPTER FIFTEEN

Cate and Landry arrived at Beau Rivage as the sun was setting, and soon they were in their usual seats on the back veranda, drinking wine and listening to the cicadas start up their nightfall chirping. They asked about Callie's husband, Jordan, with whom they'd shared an eerie adventure that became a segment called *The Nursery*.

Jordan was busy juggling his architectural practice and overseeing the Arbors, his home that was also St. Francisville's newest bed-and-breakfast. St. Francisville was a tourist destination, and the rooms in Jordan's old house were full almost every night. Callie's property lay along the river in a beautiful setting, but it was remote and off the main road and had far less traffic than Jordan's. She had a lady to help with her place, and she stayed with her husband at the Arbors most of each week.

Cate recalled when she and Landry first visited Beau Rivage, when she sat in the same chair and saw her first ghost. "Have you seen Anne-Marie lately?" she asked, but Callie hadn't. After what happened in *The Nursery*, Anne-Marie had said she wouldn't be back, and she hadn't returned.

"I miss her," Callie admitted, adding that as odd as Anne-Marie was, she had also been her protector and guardian. It made her sad to think she'd never again appear without warning and start talking in riddles.

They spent a wonderful evening catching up over dinner and wine. Afterwards, Landry asked if they could have a brandy in the library. They sat on Callie's grandmother's overstuffed couch under the stern countenance of Leonore Arceneaux, whose painting hung above the fireplace. An ancestor of Callie's, Leonore had owned the property after the Civil War and played a part in Callie's own adventures at Beau Rivage.

Unlike the last time, no ghosts roamed the halls tonight. Landry and Cate slept with the second-floor windows open to catch the calls of night birds, the wind in the trees, and the lap-lapping of the Atchafalaya River a hundred yards away.

After breakfast on the veranda, Landry left for Opelousas. He found Lee doing the same thing, sitting in his wheelchair in the front yard of the facility under a huge old oak and smoking a cigarette. A much less friendly woman than Ruby sat in a folding chair beside him. When Landry walked up, she gave him the chair and went inside so they could talk in private.

"You have your beeper," she told Lee. "Just buzz me when you're ready."

As seniors can do sometimes, Lee wanted to talk about his stay in the hospital, how many meds he was on, and how well he was doing, all things considered. Landry indulged him and then asked if they could pick up where they left off.

"Do you remember what you promised we'd talk about when I came back?"

Lee nodded. With a twinkle in his eye and a slight grin, he replied, "Do you remember what I told you to bring me when you came back?"

Landry laughed, pulled a carton of Winston cigarettes from a sack, and handed them over. "You don't forget much, do you?"

"For an old man, you mean? Naw, I'm blessed. Ninety-seven and still on top of the dirt." He put the carton in his lap and said, "What have you learned since we met in Perry?"

"After I left you, I looked through some records at the courthouse, and I stopped by the sheriff's office. He made it clear that he didn't want me nosing around town. I made one more stop, at the Hebert Funeral Home, and I got the cold shoulder there too."

"That don't surprise me. People still fret about things that happened a hundred years ago. Still keepin' secrets for no reason, if you ask me. Who cares now about somebody's granddad who did some bad things? Now tell me what you know about Billy Whistler."

Landry told Lee about the old newspaper articles and his discussion with Catfish.

Lee sucked the smoke deep into his lungs, exhaled with a cough, and said, "There's a lot that people don't know about Billy, and most folks think it's just a legend. You know about legends; they change with every tellin'. But Billy's story has two parts that never changed over all the years. One is that he first appeared on the night those fellas burned the town and somebody got lynched. And the other has to do with some girls who disappeared from time to time. I may have mentioned them earlier. People say he was the one what snatched 'em, but that may be a made-up story to make Billy seem even scarier."

Landry interrupted. "I want to hear the rest, but first let's talk about the parts that never change. Who got lynched?"

Lee looked away, like he was hedging. "Maybe one of them religious freaks."

"Could it have been one of the vigilantes?"

"You know, don't you? Somebody's told you, and maybe it *was* one of them. They had just burned the town, after all. Stands to reason those folks would be mad as a hornet."

"Did Billy Whistler kill him?"

"Billy Whistler's a legend. I told you that already."

"Lee, I think you're hiding something. You keep talking about Billy Whistler like he's real. Please tell me the story."

Although Lee disparaged others for keeping secrets, he had kept this one for so long he couldn't look Landry in the eyes. His voice dropped to a raspy whisper. "Mr. Auguste Dauphin was the man's name. He done somethin' awful that night, and the Sons of Jehovah hanged him for it. There's one body that'll never be found."

"Because he became Billy Whistler?"

Lee snorted. "Hell no, son! God, you've got this story all mixed up. I done told you what the man did. He committed a grave offense against them people."

Frustrated, Landry fought for patience. He was having to draw out every answer. "Did he kill one of them?"

"Might have been better if he had." He took another long drag from his cigarette and said, "Enough about him. Now I'm gonna tell you about Billy Whistler."

"One second. Can we talk first about the girls who disappeared over the years?"

Now Lee seemed frustrated. "I never saw anybody ask as many questions as you do. If you can be quiet for a minute, I'll tell you the story like it was told to me, and you'll hear all about the girls."

The old man skipped the beginning of Billy Whistler's story because it involved Auguste Dauphin. He should never have said that name, and he had to be careful now.

"Just so you know, nobody's ever proved this story I'm tellin' you. Some people swear by it. It's become kind of real to me, because I've heard it for almost ninety-seven years, long enough for it to sound real. Ain't nobody ever captured him, or met him face-to-face, or nothin' like that. Sightings, stories, scary tales, that kind of stuff. Same as the rougarou stories — some people even say Billy Whistler's one of them. We talked about them last time, remember?"

Landry nodded.

"Here's my take on it. Billy Whistler's a ghoul who's lived for over a hundred years. He was alive in 1880, and he's still alive today, if alive is what he is. Maybe he's one of them walking corpses like a zombie or something, and then again maybe he truly is a rougarou. People say he died and the Sons of Jehovah buried him in a grave somewhere, but his grave is empty because he still roams the earth. Ever hear of Remembering Day?"

"Yes," Landry said, but he didn't know what it meant.

"It's all part of the same legend. The story goes that every ten years, on the anniversary of Asher's being burned down, the cult holds an all-night vigil where the town used to be. It's called Remembering Day, on account of they remember when the vigilantes came. They dance around and do who-knows-what to each other. Billy Whistler comes out on those nights and sacrifices a girl. Crazy story, ain't it?"

"That's what you meant about girls disappearing?"

"Yep."

"Missing kids are a huge deal. Where were they from, and why aren't their families still looking for them?"

"They were from Abbeville, far as I know. As to their families, maybe they did. Guess Sheriff Conreco would know about that. Why don't you ask him?" He took another puff.

"Why doesn't the sheriff go to Asher on Remembering Day and investigate?"

Lee grinned. "I told you about them secrets people still keep." He stretched and yawned and said, "Man, I'm beat."

Landry was far from finished with this subject, but his time was almost up. There was one more thing he wanted to learn before he left.

"I first came to Abbeville because of a strange voicemail someone left at my station." He pulled up the message on his phone and read it verbatim. "I'd like to help her, but with so little information, I don't know where to begin."

Without hesitation the old man said, "Paulie. I'd start with him. If there's anything worth knowing around this parish, he's the man to talk to."

"Paulie? Paulie who? Where can I find him?"

Lee was fading. He pulled the fob from his pocket and clicked it. "I have to go inside now. I'm gettin' tired and I need my nap. Been nice talkin' to you again, and thanks for the cigarettes. You come back anytime you want."

As the nurse came across the lawn, Landry pushed for more. "Please, Lee, tell me who Paulie is and where to find him."

Lee's eyelids were fluttering now. "Paulie? Everybody knows who he is. He's at the church."

"The church in Abbeville? The Catholic church?"

The nurse came to his side. "Ready to go in, Mr. Lee?"

"Yeah, I'm pooped! Landry, you come back and see me now, you hear?"

Who was Paulie, and where was he? Landry sat in the parking lot and searched the internet. Lee had lived in Perry his entire life, but that tiny town had no churches. The largest church in the parish, Saint Mary Magdalene in Abbeville, was just two miles away, but there was no one on staff named Paul or Paulie. And it might not even be a staff person he was looking for. Paulie might be someone who worshipped there — a faithful member of the flock. If it wasn't a clergyman, Landry faced going to every church in the parish to look for someone named Paul.

Crossing his fingers, he searched for parish clergymen named Paul and found two. Both were priests, one in a small church in Abbeville and one ten miles away in Kaplan.

He called the Kaplan church and spoke with Father Paul Ambrose, who had served the congregation for two years after moving from Shreveport. He had never heard of Lee Alard and had never heard of Asher.

Father Paul Broussard, the one in Abbeville, was out for a few hours. Landry left his number and checked in with Cate, who said she and Callie were driving to Lafayette for a late lunch at Prejean's. He said he'd join them and turned south to pick up the Evangeline Thruway. Prejean's was a classic Cajun restaurant frequented by locals and tourists alike. Even at two p.m. it was busy, and he got one of the only available parking spots.

An enormous stuffed alligator greeted him just inside the door, its yawning mouth flashing sharp teeth. Cate waved from across the room. Just as he joined them and ordered a beer, his phone rang.

He stepped to the lobby to take the call. It was Father Paul Broussard, asking how he could help.

Landry explained he was an investigative reporter, and the priest laughed. "I don't think you need an introduction, Mr. Drake. What's this about?"

"I had a visit with Lee Alard. He mentioned I should talk to Paulie, but we got cut short, and I didn't get anything else. By chance are you Paulie?"

"I am! Mr. Lee — gosh, how's he doing? I haven't seen him in a couple of years. I've known him since I was a kid. I was little Paulie Broussard to him, and I guess I always will be."

Landry asked if he could come to Abbeville tomorrow, and the priest agreed, adding that he was looking forward to meeting Landry and hearing what he was up to in the parish. Since it was Sunday, they agreed to meet at the church after noon Mass.

He returned to Cate and Callie, ordered an oyster po'boy, and filled them in on his trip to Opelousas. He told Cate they would have to leave earlier tomorrow than they'd planned. "I just set up an interview in Abbeville at one. When it's over, I'll drop you at the Lafayette airport before I drive home."

Callie insisted on taking Cate to Lafayette herself. It made better sense; once Landry was finished in Abbeville, he could go on to New Orleans instead of backtracking for an hour.

"I'm still worried about you going there," Cate said, explaining to Callie that he was persona non grata in Vermilion Parish. He promised to make the visit quick, to stay under the radar and out of trouble. The girls laughed.

After lunch they drove to St. Francisville and spent the afternoon with Callie's husband, Jordan Blanchard, and his daughters. The improvements Jordan had made to the B&B that had once been his home office were impressive. Cate and Landry lingered for a long time in the nursery, the room where Jordan's girls had disappeared. As they stood in the bright, sunny room, they remarked on how different it was today than when Jordan first opened the door. For fifty years no one had been inside — it was dark, gloomy and filled with ancient toys. The room and its eerie occupant had drawn his children into a sequence of horrifying events.

Something positive came from their experiences. After going through hell in this room, Callie and Jordan had emerged knowing they were meant to be together. Their bond was strengthened when Anne-Marie, the child ghost who once saved Callie's life, stepped in to facilitate the return of Jordan's missing children. Had she not agreed to help, Jordan would never have seen them again.

They decided on an early dinner before the three of them drove back to Beau Rivage, and everyone got a kick out of Landry's suggestion they eat at the River View. It was a low-end dive on a dead-end road where Landry had gone looking for information. It was a lot of things, but not the place for their dinner.

They drove to an outstanding little seafood restaurant on the False River in New Roads, just down the road and across the Mississippi from St. Francisville. Landry brought Jordan up to speed on his work in Vermilion Parish, mentioning the voicemail that got everything started, what his research had turned up so far, and how almost everyone in Abbeville was friendly. Except for the sheriff and the undertaker. Jordan wondered what that was about, and Landry repeated what Lee had told him — some people keep secrets for a long, long time.

"There's something going on, and it involves Asher," he added as the food came and they prepared to dive in to their sizzling dishes. "The more they try to run me off, the more I wonder what it is."

"Don't forget what curiosity did to the cat," Cate replied.

He looked at her and grinned, but she wasn't smiling.

As the sun set and the tree frogs down by the water began their nightly trills, they reminisced about friendship, adventure and good times ahead. After a scrumptious meal, two bottles of wine, and a shared slab of mile-high cake, Jordan drove back to St. Francisville, and the others returned to Beau Rivage.

CHAPTER SIXTEEN

The tower bells of the little church pealed, signaling the end of Mass. From the parking lot, Landry watched the priest and his parishioners come through the front doors, shaking hands and gathering in small groups to chat, as good friends do.

The cleric was tall, with wavy black hair and a kind demeanor. He gave everyone a warm smile and spoke with them. Landry knew they'd be complimenting him on the sermon or asking about his health, or just chatting with the leader of the flock.

Church had been a big part of his life as a youth, and he sometimes felt something was missing now that he didn't attend. He had prayed many times for God's help in a tough situation. God always came through, but somehow Landry accepted the help, offering nothing in return.

He approached the priest, maintaining a respectful distance until the last people finished talking. *He's not much older than I am,* Landry thought.

"Father Broussard? I'm Landry Drake."

"It's just Paul. I saw you walking from the parking lot. It's an honor to have you here, and I can't wait to find out what's up."

The priest said his office was too small for visits. Even the confessional was bigger, he laughed. He suggested lunch at the RiverFront, and soon they were at an outside table overlooking the Vermilion River, with two glasses of Pinot Noir and bowls of okra gumbo on the way.

Landry explained how following Lee Alard's cryptic references to Paulie and the church had led him here. The priest explained he'd been little Paulie Broussard to everyone in Perry when he was growing up. For some, the nickname never went away, even when he chose the priesthood. He inquired about Lee's health, and Landry told him about his visits and that the old man was in a facility in Opelousas now.

They talked about what brought Landry to Abbeville. "It started with an anonymous voicemail someone left with our station manager. The girl sounded afraid for her life, Father. Lee Alard said if anybody knew what was going on in this parish, it would be you."

A shadow moved across Father Paul's face. His voice dropped, and Landry had to lean in to hear him. "I wish I could help you, but I'm afraid you've come to the wrong person. I'm sorry to waste your time; if you wish, we can cancel our lunch order so you can get back to New Orleans."

In an instant his cordiality was gone.

"That's fine. We can talk about other things. Growing up in Perry, I'm sure you listened to stories about Billy Whistler and the cult, even if you don't know anything about the girl who called."

It took a long time for his reply, and he had a pained expression on his face when he spoke. "I didn't say I knew nothing about the girl. I said I wish I could help you."

"So you do know?"

Another long pause. "I'm a priest, Landry. There are things I'm required to hold in confidence."

"Are you talking about confessions?"

He nodded. "Not just that. You can't ask more of me than I can give."

At that moment a hand clamped down on Landry's shoulder and squeezed hard.

"Well, well, look who's back in town. The famous ghost hunter." Sheriff Conreco looked out of place in a coat and tie. He'd been to church and chosen the same restaurant for lunch. And he'd spotted Landry, which wasn't good.

"Hello, Sheriff," the priest said with a smile.

Conreco nodded respectfully. "Father, you're in mighty poor company. This fellow here isn't welcome in Vermilion Parish. In fact, I told him I'd lock him up if I saw him here again. Didn't I, Mr. Drake?"

"That's what you said, although I still haven't heard on what grounds you intend to arrest me."

The sheriff looked at his watch. "You've got fifteen minutes. If you're still here, you and I are going to the station."

Father Paul didn't understand. "Sheriff, has Mr. Drake committed a crime? If he has, why haven't you arrested him already? And if he hasn't, what's the big deal? We're not in the Wild West, are we? Is this town not big enough for the both of you?"

The priest smiled, but Junior wasn't happy. He wasn't accustomed to being challenged; he was the law in a small town, and people did what he commanded. Truth was, he had no cause to hold the reporter. He simply wanted the problem gone.

He pointed his finger at the priest and growled, "Watch what you say to him, Father. You're not part of this, and trust me, you don't want to be. Stay away from this nosy little pissant." He turned and walked back to a table where his wife waited.

As lunch arrived, other diners pointed and whispered. The sheriff's visit to their table had caught people's attention. They looked over and realized who Landry was.

Father Paul asked what was wrong with the sheriff, and Landry explained. He listened without commenting until both Landry's story and their meals were finished.

"There are secrets in this parish," he said after Landry settled the check. "You're getting too close for some people's comfort. I'm not sure how you've been received in other places, but things work differently here. My advice is that you find another story. A few people have kept things under wraps for more than a hundred years. You can't understand —" He paused, unsure what else to say. "This goes far deeper than you can imagine, that's all I'm saying."

"You're telling me to let this story go? What about that terrified girl who said she'd be dead if 'they' found out she called? Are you willing to risk that happening, when you could help? Who are 'they,' and why does it matter after all this time? As you said, it's been over a hundred years. Don't you care about the poor girl's welfare? She's reaching out for help, and there's something you aren't telling me."

The priest stood and walked Landry out of the restaurant without a word. Only when they reached the parking lot did he answer.

"You ask why it matters? It matters because it isn't over, and it may never be. I care very much about the girl's welfare. I said earlier there are things I cannot tell you. Let this go while you can. Once things settle down, everything will be fine."

"This isn't right, Father. How can you live with yourself? You could be part of the solution, but you're choosing to let the bad things continue."

Father Paul nodded. "As God is my witness, I want to make things right. For your own sake, I implore you to drop this now. If you insist on continuing, I'll contact her. If — and that's a big if — she agrees to talk, I'll call you. Don't count on it and promise me you'll let it go if she won't talk to you."

"It's the right thing to do, even if only for her sake. And, Father, I can't promise you anything. The less you tell me, the more intrigued I am."

"Don't say I didn't warn you. You hold Pandora's box in your hands. If you open the lid, you'll never close it again."

CHAPTER SEVENTEEN

After meeting Landry, Father Paul prayed for God's guidance. What should he do? Landry had a point. Em had left a voicemail asking for help, and he knew why, because he knew a great deal about her. He thought back to that odd day recently when they first met.

He had entered the confession box, and a thin black curtain separated him from the person on the other side. She cleared her throat several times and shuffled her feet, but she hadn't spoken. He made the Sign of the Cross and began. "In the name of the Father —"

"Crap!" she yelled. "I didn't know there was somebody over there!"

He pulled back the curtain and saw a teenaged girl wearing a torn homemade dress. She had matted hair and a face streaked with dirt. She looked frightened and frazzled.

"Are you — are you hiding from somebody too?" she asked in a whisper.

"Hiding? Is that why you came?"

"Yes, sir. Is this your house? I tried the door, and I came in to find someplace to rest."

"This is a church, child, the house of God. Haven't you ever been in a church?"

"No, sir."

He pressed her, asking who she ran away from, but she wouldn't answer. Then he said, "This is a confessional, a place where you can talk to God through me. Do you want to confess your sins?"

"I ain't the one who sinned, sir. The others did, and they'll kill me if they find out I told anyone."

Father Paul wasn't sure what to do. Many people hesitated to tell private things during first confessions, but there was something heartbreaking in the girl's words. He had a feeling whatever she confessed would be something his training hadn't prepared him for.

He took her to his cramped office because he thought it important to talk to her face-to-face. She resisted at first but then gave in. The child needed help, and he hoped he could give it to her.

She said her name was Em. When he asked her last name, she didn't know for sure. Savary maybe, or Lafont. It had to be one or the other, she said. She thought for a moment and said, "I think it's Savary." Her ragged clothes and men's running shoes a size too large made her look like an escapee from a refugee camp.

"Em. That's a nice name. Is it short for Emily?"

"It ain't short for nothin'."

He said he didn't understand, and she explained, "My name's M. Just M. The girls' names are just letters. Only men get real names. You know that, right?"

He shook his head and wondered where on earth this girl came from. It seemed she'd dropped in from another place — a time warp, or a *Twilight Zone* episode — and had just dropped into his confessional. She spoke English in an uneducated, country way, but every word from her lips was bizarre and unreal.

M, she explained, was the thirteenth letter of the alphabet, although he doubted she knew the alphabet. She was the thirteenth child born in her birth year, so they called her M.

"I don't understand. Where are you from?"

"New Asher. Elder Johnson Lafont's the leader."

"I've never heard of it. Where is it?"

"Where the commune is. I ran away last night because they were going to punish me."

He learned that after lights out at nine p.m. yesterday, she sneaked away from a town hidden deep in a forest near a bayou. She'd never been away, but several of the boys had been to another place – a bigger town where the elder and his deacons bought supplies with the elder and his deacons. Those boys told stories about how different things were in the outside world.

She found a highway and followed it north throughout the night, hiding in the trees every time a vehicle approached. After a long walk she came to Abbeville, a larger and more frightening place than she'd ever seen. Father Paul tried to put himself in her shoes. Her town had wooden buildings and houses, but Abbeville was filled with structures, each bright with electricity. And there were cars, trucks and people everywhere.

She walked into town as the sun rose, and she hid under the church. Like many buildings in the flood-prone parish, the church sat on concrete pylons that raised it a foot off the ground. She crawled underneath and slept, awakening when she heard him open the church doors. She sneaked inside, saw him dusting the sanctuary, and hid in the confessional where he found her.

He wanted to ask why she believed people were out to kill her, but first there were basic needs to attend to. She was hungry, dusty and exhausted, and he enlisted the matronly church secretary to find her clean clothes and shoes from the clothes closet. The lady showed her to the bathroom and taught her how to use the toilet, sink and shower that the church had installed for the homeless people. After getting over her astonishment about how water came from a pipe in the wall, she took a long hot shower.

She emerged fresh and clean, and Father Paul said he'd take her to a restaurant for breakfast. She had never heard of a restaurant, and when she learned it involved leaving the church, she refused to go outside because "they" might be waiting. He went instead, returning with eggs, bacon, buttered toast and hash browns, all of which she ate ravenously, using her fingers more than the spoon, the only utensil she recognized.

She seemed comfortable talking to him, although each little noise from outside his office startled her. She told her story, one that would have sounded outlandish if this pitiful waif hadn't been sitting next to him. He believed her because he felt she wasn't capable of lying.

Although vigilantes wiped out Asher, that wasn't the end of things. The Sons of Jehovah simply moved away and built another town — New Asher. She described her trip from the town to Abbeville, and he decided it might lie in the woods south of Delcambre and near Bayou Carlin.

Cult member last names were either Lafont or Savary. She thought she was a Savary, but as she explained further, he understood why she didn't know for sure.

He pushed for details of how the cult worked. If your last name was Lafont, she said, you could only marry a Savary. Father Paul assumed they used this method to avoid intermarriage, although after fourteen decades of communal living, it was unlikely that solved the problem.

Em explained that she just turned eighteen, the time for her to breed. It was a ritual that perpetuated the colony. She was given to one of Elder Lafont's cousins, or perhaps a nephew — it would have been impossible to draw a family tree from this convolution of relatives — but she hadn't conceived. Another Lafont took a turn and had the same result. Barren women were a useless burden, and what lay ahead terrified her.

Father Paul controlled himself as she talked, although it was difficult when the tales were so barbaric and unbelievable in twenty-first-century America. Em had known other girls who couldn't have children, and one day they'd just disappear. One was an older friend, although friendships weren't encouraged in the commune, and she had asked her father what happened to her.

He had laughed and said, "Guess they gave her to Billy Whistler, since she wasn't no use to us anymore." His words terrified her — a barren child meant nothing more to him than if they'd given away a dog.

"And that's why I ran away," she said as Father Paul stared in shock. "I wasn't no use to them either."

Not only did she relate an unbelievable story, she might also have validated that the legendary Billy Whistler really existed.

CHAPTER EIGHTEEN

Back in his apartment that evening, Landry called Cate to be sure she had gotten home. She asked about Abbeville and he told her only part of what had happened. He'd met the priest, gone to lunch with him, and they discussed the mysterious voicemail. Father Paul couldn't say much because some of what he knew, he'd learned in the sanctity of the confession box.

He left out his confrontation with Sheriff Conreco and the priest's strong suggestion that he back off a story that became odder and more puzzling with each clue he uncovered.

She asked what was next.

"I'm going back. I want to spend some time where the town of Asher used to be. I'll rent a boat and go down the river."

"I want to come with you."

He hadn't expected that response, and he considered it a bad idea. Something was wrong at Asher; after talking to the priest, he was more certain than ever. What if something went wrong? What about the sheriff's threat? Cate had no business going with him.

"I don't think you should. The voicemail says something bad is going on and that the cult is still around. If that's true, it could be dangerous."

"Then why are you going?"

"Because I have to find out."

"Are you going to use the same guide?"

He really hoped to rent Catfish's boat and go alone.

"Possibly, but there's really no reason to use him. I know how to get there. Why pay him to sit there and wait?"

"Okay, it's settled. When do you want to go?"

"Friday," he said, hoping that day wouldn't work for her.

"Done deal. I'll meet you at the Lafayette airport Friday. Same flight as last time."

He met her on Friday, and the next morning they drove to Perry. Catfish grinned as Landry and a beautiful girl with raven-black hair pulled back in a ponytail walked into his place. He put down his magazine, took his feet off the desk, and said, "Welcome back! I hoped you wouldn't wait long! What's it been — two weeks?"

Landry laughed. "Yeah. I missed you so much I couldn't spend another day without you!"

"You're working on a TV show, right? Has to be, 'cause you're back so soon. You're famous, man. Why didn't you tell me I had a celebrity in my boat?"

Landry presumed he'd found out who Landry was from the sheriff. Catfish seemed to be a genuine individual, and if Junior had somehow learned that the guide took him downriver, Landry figured Catfish would have answered his questions honestly.

"My celebrity status never came up. Besides, I didn't want you hounding me for an autograph."

Catfish belched a laugh. "Who's your guest? Planning to show her beautiful downtown Asher?"

"This is my friend Cate Adams. We're back because I wanted to spend a few hours floating downstream on a peaceful river. There's no reason to return to Asher; I didn't find anything last time. I'd just like to rent your boat."

Catfish thought if he had a girlfriend that looked like Cate, he'd want some privacy too. "Can you handle a boat and motor?"

"I grew up on the bayou in Jeanerette. My dad had one, and I was on Bayou Teche all summer long."

"Never rented the boat by itself before. Where are you all headed?"

"Nowhere special, like I said. I packed a cooler, and we'll find someplace to have a picnic lunch. We'll be back by midafternoon — three at the latest."

He thought for a moment and said, "Sure, why not? You remember from last time the motor can be cantankerous, but you'll be fine. I'll give you my number. If anything goes wrong, I'll send somebody down to get you."

They loaded the picnic basket, pulled out into the river, and headed south. Catfish stood on the dock. Once they were out of sight, he made the call.

"Landry Drake just rented my boat. Him and a girl, heading south toward Asher."

———

The leafy branches of tall oak trees shaded much of the bayou, and Cate removed her jacket to enjoy what sun there was. She commented that she learned new things about him every day, such as the fact that his father once had a boat.

"That's not entirely true," he admitted. "One of my friend's fathers had a boat, and we took it out once or twice. I never ran it myself, but how hard can it be? Even if we sank, the shore's just over there. It's not like we're on the Mississippi."

"I'm sure you can handle it, cap'n. My, look at the time! It's almost eleven. I think I'll have a glass of wine. Would you like one?"

That sounded just perfect. They'd packed a nice Pinot Grigio with a screw top, and she dug out two plastic stemmed glasses. After a toast, she settled back to enjoy the ride.

"That's where we're coming back to," he pointed out as they drifted past Asher. "There's no place for a picnic there, so let's keep going until we find a good spot."

He found the perfect place a few miles downstream. It had a small sandy beach and plenty of shade. He tied the boat to a tree and unloaded the cooler while Cate spread a blanket.

They ate without conversation; it had been a while since they had been alone, and it was nice just to spend the day together. Landry decided he'd made the right decision not to tell her everything. Right here, right now, things were perfect; it seemed as if nothing could go wrong on a beautiful Saturday like this one.

When she was finished packing up, he suggested they should do one more thing before leaving. He explained and she exclaimed, "Right here? What if someone comes along?"

"Have you seen another boat? If we hear anyone coming, they can watch!"

Anyone on the river could see their boat tied off and them as well, but even with no traffic, it was exciting. "Okay, I'm game! Get your clothes off!"

Afterwards they lay naked on the blanket, listening to the melodic whirring of insects, a sound he'd grown up with and that he missed. It was idyllic, and he told her he wouldn't trade this time for anything.

Back on the river before one, he guided the boat to shore at Asher, tied it off, and helped her through the fence. It surprised her how big the town must have been.

Keeping an ear cocked for Billy Whistler, he took dozens of pictures, and she helped measure off city blocks to create a basic layout of the town. Landry didn't know what Billy's warble sounded like. Catfish said he'd heard it, but the man had had way more than a six-pack by then. For all Landry knew, Billy Whistler might have been crooning "Moon River" in Catfish's head.

Today there came a cacophony of chirping from birds in the trees overhead and others far away, so if Billy began warbling, Landry doubted he could discern it.

He took her down the path. A few headstones sticking up in the weeds provided the first clue they were in a cemetery. He'd looked for inscriptions last time, but if there had ever been writing, it was gone now. Today they were just rocks with crude rounded tops. She found other stones — rectangular flat ones flush with the ground. The plot was far larger than he'd thought; she made a quick count and came up with seventy-one stones that might be markers.

As he snapped pictures, Landry noticed boot prints. Someone — maybe two people — had been here recently.

He saw two stones lying next to each other.

JAMES SAVARY MARCH 2009

K SAVARY JAN 2007

"Look, Cate! This cemetery's still being used — at least it was ten years ago. These are cult members — they're all named Lafont or Savary. The Sons of Jehovah can't be that far away." Although it might result in nothing, he had two names and dates to check at the courthouse.

In their cursory walkabout, they found no other stones with complete inscriptions and no readable dates, and he proclaimed he was done.

Back on shore, she gathered the blanket while he picked up the cooler. Landry was loading the boat when Cate stifled a scream. A tall man stood in the trees. He wore a badge on a khaki shirt whose buttons struggled to contain the man's gut. Landry glanced toward the river; he'd missed seeing the man's boat until now.

"Well, hello, Mr. Drake. We meet again."

This confirmed that Catfish had ratted him out, which was no surprise. Landry was not only an outsider, he was an investigative reporter on the sheriff's shit list. He went for the offense because he'd done nothing wrong. He still didn't believe Conreco would have the nerve to arrest him for being in the parish.

"Sheriff, fancy meeting you here. Out for a spin on the river?"

"Don't smart-talk me, boy. Did you tell this lady here she was in for a surprise if you came back to my parish? Or did you figure I was just jokin' with you when I talked to you Sunday at lunch with Father Paul?"

Irritated, Landry snapped, "Are you harassing me, Sheriff?"

Conreco laughed. "Naw, I wouldn't call it harassment. I'm investigating a crime, and I found you two right here at the scene. I told you to stay away, mister reporter. Now both of you are in big trouble. Grand larceny's a serious offense."

"Grand larceny?" Cate cried. "What are you talking about?"

"I'm talking about you all stealin' this here boat."

CHAPTER NINETEEN

The sheriff had come prepared; he'd brought two sets of handcuffs. He cuffed them and put them in his boat. Landry thought Conreco wouldn't arrest Cate. This trumped-up charge involved him, not her. As they motored upstream, he gave Cate the number of the lawyer he'd contacted earlier and told her what to do.

They pulled in to Catfish's dock, and Junior helped Cate out, leaving Landry struggling to get off the boat with his hands cuffed behind his back.

Embarrassed, Catfish ran to the boat to help Landry, but Junior waved him off. "That's my prisoner, son. You stay away from him."

With some effort, Landry plopped onto the dock and stood.

The sheriff walked them to his squad car and removed Cate's cuffs. He told Landry to give her his phone and car keys and said she'd better be glad he was in a good mood. Otherwise he'd have charged her as an accessory.

Grand larceny. Landry laughed at the thought. That tub of shit wasn't worth a hundred bucks. Even if they had stolen it, this was no case of grand larceny. As Conreco put him in the back seat, he saw Cate making the call.

Twenty minutes later, he waited in a processing room when a local attorney hired by Landry's lawyer came in. He said the sheriff would drop the matter if Landry agreed to leave the parish and not return.

Landry had expected this. It was more than repressing journalistic freedom or denying First Amendment rights. He had work to do here, and he was determined to find out what the sheriff had to do with Asher.

"No way. I didn't steal the boat. The sheriff's hiding something, and I intend to find out what it is."

"That's your call. You're entitled to do what you want, but there's something else. He says he'll arrest the girl too."

"Seriously? She's an accessory to grand larceny? All this is pure harassment."

"No, sir, it's more serious than that. He's threatened to charge her with indecent exposure. He says you all were naked on the shoreline and you engaged in a sex act. He has pictures to prove it."

Son of a bitch! He'd been there all along!

That changed things. This battle could be fought another time. He'd get both of them out of here, and then he'd decide what to do next. All he knew for certain was that his investigation would keep right on going.

"That was a quick trip to the pokey," she quipped as he got in the car. The lawyer had asked her to stay outside, so she wasn't aware of Conreco's threat. For now he'd leave it that way.

"I told you something was fishy with the sheriff. The more they try to stop me, the more determined I am to find out who they're protecting and what they're covering up."

She understood this man, and his reaction didn't surprise her. She warned him again to watch himself. He was in a place where he had no friends, despite how affable the townspeople appeared. She added, "Even as friendly as Catfish seems, he's in on this too."

"Let's just see what's up with old Catfish." He picked up his phone.

The poor man couldn't have been more apologetic. "Junior got to me, man. He was looking to find whoever took you down there last time, and I had to promise I'd call if you showed up again. He said it had to do with some criminal case. I felt so bad seeing you all in cuffs; there was no call for him to do that. I was embarrassed and I can't imagine how it was for you."

"I'm not embarrassed. I'm damned mad. And more determined than before. What is it about Asher, Catfish? What are people trying to hide? Is this about those men who burned the town? It's been a hundred and forty years, for God's sake. Why's it important after all that time?"

His mind swirling with crazy thoughts, Catfish took a pull on his beer and struggled to come up with an answer to throw Landry off.

"Catfish, are you still there?"

He gave up. "Yeah, yeah, I'm still here. I'm not sure what to say. We had a good trip down there, you and me, and I'm sorry about what happened today. But this is my home, Mr. Landry. Know what I mean? You can go back to Nawlins, but I live here with them. It ain't fair to make your problem my problem."

Landry understood. He let Catfish off the proverbial hook and said he hoped to see him again someday. As they drove back, he asked Cate what she thought. She could look at things objectively, and maybe she had fresh ideas. He told her everything this time — the sheriff's aggressive behavior, the indecent exposure threat, the priest's admission that there were dark secrets, and his warning not to open a Pandora's box.

They talked through the situation and came to the same conclusion. People still kept a secret from the 1800s. What was it, and why was it so important?

As they talked, he was already planning his next trip to Vermilion Parish.

CHAPTER TWENTY

Elder Johnson Lafont sat in his usual spot behind a hand-hewn oak table in the council house. Six other men, each chosen by the elder — were at the table too, and in front of them stood two people: Micah and B Savary.

The nervous couple fidgeted while the men whispered. Micah and B had received a summons, a command that meant trouble for them. Coming before the council often resulted in punishment for some alleged transgression against the Sons of Jehovah.

Micah and his wife knew why they were here. It was not for a personal transgression, but they would bear the blame.

The leader rapped the table with a gavel and the room was silent. "Where is your daughter, Deacon Micah?" His deep voice boomed like God's wrath from Heaven.

He hung his head as his wife took his hand. "Perhaps she ran away, Elder."

"*Perhaps* she ran away? She is your property and therefore your responsibility. How can you not *know* where she is?"

His wife raised her head and stammered, "Sir, she's not a bad girl."

"Silence, woman! You will not speak unless I order it. Deacon Micah, if you have any idea where or why M has gone, reveal it now or face the wrath of the council!"

"Elder, we could not have known her thoughts. Perhaps her inability to conceive was too shameful for her to bear. She cannot have gone far."

"Micah, your opinion means nothing to me. You failed to control your offspring and the consequences may even now be causing harm to our group. That should be too shameful for *you* to bear."

He stood and said, "Council, I recommend giving Deacon Micah over to Billy Whistler. What say you?"

Ayes from every man at the table, just like always. No one ever challenged the elder for fear they'd be next.

B screamed as she hugged her husband. "Please, Elder! We will look for her! Don't do this to Micah!"

"I am doing nothing to your husband. The consequences of his inaction are his to bear, and his alone. You can still conceive, so you shall remain with us for now. *We* will look for your daughter M, Sister, and *we* will find her. When we do, she will become an example. Everyone will see what happens to those who try to leave. Take him away!"

Two men in the back of the room came forward, pushed the woman to the floor, and dragged Micah out of the council house. Because she could still bear children, B had not met the fate of her husband. She would be given to another deacon while M was missing. If the girl returned, B could only imagine what fate awaited her and her child.

They had taken her husband away, and his screams echoed through the forest that night. She felt sadness for his pain, but she didn't even shed a tear over the loss of their relationship. In the Sons of Jehovah women were chattel, used for a man's pleasure and for procreating. She and Micah never had an emotional attachment.

Her daughter M was a different story. They had a bond, and it tore at her heart to think she might never see M again. But she hoped that was how it would be. The girl would pay a terrible price if they brought her back.

Deep in the woods, Billy Whistler toyed with his new prize. He would rather it had been a girl — in his primitive state, strange feelings stirred when he captured one. The men were just for play, and his twisted face broke into a grotesque grin every time he clawed Deacon Micah's skin and heard him scream in pain.

He wanted to keep this going for as long as possible, but it always had to end. The elder made him return the bodies because he wanted to bury them, so tomorrow he'd drag Micah's corpse back to New Asher.

CHAPTER TWENTY-ONE

Father Paul hadn't spoken to his sister, Valerie, in several days. As always, he was worried until she confirmed Em was okay. They talked about other things a moment, and he asked to speak with the girl.

"Hello?" The voice was hesitant, as Father Paul remembered it from the day they met.

"Hi, Em. How are things going?"

"Tell me the password so I'm sure it's you." Scared. Shaky. Trusting no one, taking nothing for granted, not even a familiar voice.

"It's me, Em. The password is chicory. We need to talk for a moment."

"Oh God. Everything's all right, isn't it? Please, Father, tell me everything's all right."

"All good. Nothing's changed. Stay calm. You're safe."

Her voice quivered. "If they find me, they'll kill me for telling you what I did. They'll kill you too."

"Is Valerie taking good care of you?"

"Yes, but I can't go outdoors. If I went out there, someone might recognize me. What if they're already here, waiting for me —"

He stopped her with a gentle word. "She's my sister, Em. I told you there's no one on earth I trust more than Val, and you can trust her too."

He saw that Em's state of mind had not improved one iota since he'd taken her to New Orleans two weeks ago. He said he had good news — there was someone who might help her.

The tension was palpable. "Have you told them about me?"

"Of course not. I explained to you that a priest can't reveal anything. I'm also your friend and I care about you. I'm on your side and you can trust me."

She was wary. "How are you sure someone can help me if you didn't tell?"

"Okay, let me explain. You left a voicemail at a TV station in New Orleans."

"Crap. How did you find that out?"

"Because of the story you told me when we met at the church. A man who works at the TV station told me what was in the voicemail, and I knew it was you. Which brings up a question — how did you make a phone call, and how did you learn about TV? You said there's nothing modern in New Asher."

"Elder Johnson has a phone for emergencies; one of his daughters is my friend G. We snuck it out one time and we messed with it. He'd printed some numbers on the back. Nine-one-one. When we pressed those numbers, a woman began talking. I knew right then if something happened to me, I'd ask that woman for help.

"I found out about TV from my brother Jed. Sometimes he goes with the deacons to town to buy supplies. He told me about all the stuff we don't have. He watched the news on a TV at the Walmart, and there were people helping a man who had been trapped. I was trapped too, ever since I was old enough for them to use me. I memorized the name of the TV place. Its name was Channel Nine in New

Orleans. I used Elder Johnson's phone when he was gone to town, the lady helped me talk to Channel Nine, and I left a message. That's all I did, but now they found you! Father, I'm scared. Do they know where I am? If you tell anybody — anybody — Elder Johnson will find out!"

Father Paul tried to ease her anxiety. "The person I talked to helps people like the one your brother told you about." He explained the convoluted way in which Landry Drake had connected the dots. Through a combination of good investigative reporting and luck, he had come to Abbeville, and now he wanted to talk to the person who left the voicemail.

"No, no, no, no, no! I never wanted them to find me! I wanted them to go see what was happening."

"He's done that. He's been here more than once. Your message brought him here, but people threatened him. They told him to get out of town, and that made him want to help more. I think you should meet him. It can't hurt you; he's an honest man, and I believe he'll do whatever you say. I'll be there too if you wish."

"Why do I have to meet him? I don't want to!"

"You've been through enough, and that's why this is so important. This has to stop. It took guts for you to leave a message, and it worked. Someone came to help, but only you can show him what to do."

"You know what will happen to me if they find out."

"They won't, Em. I'll protect you and so will he. Do you want to live in fear the rest of your life, always hiding and being afraid? When this is over, you'll be free."

She didn't answer for a moment. "You believe you can protect me, but you can't. Whether I talk to the man or not, if they find me, I'm dead. And they *will* find me. I know they will. So I'll talk to him."

CHAPTER TWENTY-TWO

Cate called on Wednesday and asked what his weekend looked like. Catching up on chores he'd neglected while he was out of town, he replied, and when she offered to fly over after work on Friday, he was ecstatic.

"I'll grab an Uber," she said. "Let's have a romantic weekend. I'll stay until Monday to give us two full days."

He suggested they meet in the lobby bar of the Royal Sonesta Hotel on Bourbon Street. The dark, cozy venue had live music and great cocktails. It sounded perfect and she asked if they could go to GW Fins for dinner.

"Hard place to get into on a Friday night with two days' notice," he responded, but she shot back that she knew a famous television personality who could pull strings just by dropping his name.

He laughed because they'd been there a few times. She was aware Landry knew the maître d', and reserving a quiet table for two would be easy for him.

"Seven p.m. at the Royal Sonesta," she said. "Love you and can't wait to see you."

On Friday evening he saw her walking through the lobby. As she approached the table, he rose and gave her a hug and kiss. They raised their glasses, settled back, and talked quietly as the band set up. Just then Landry's phone rang. He'd forgotten to mute it, and he started to turn it off, but he stopped when he saw it was Father Paul Broussard.

The priest called rarely, so he thought it had to be important. He apologized, stepped out, and returned the call. Five minutes later he was back and she sensed his excitement.

"What's going on?"

"The girl I told you about — the one who left the voicemail — she's agreed to talk to me. Father Paul set it up. He says I need to jump on this because if she has much time to think about it, she may back out."

"Do you need to go now?"

"Not tonight. Tomorrow, but I won't be gone long."

"Can I come along?"

"I wouldn't want to spook her, and so your being there might help. Another girl and that kind of thing. Yeah, let's go together, but if she says you can't stay —"

She grinned. "I'll get the hint I'm not wanted. I'm your partner in crime; I wore the handcuffs to prove it. I'd like to meet her and hear her story."

He called the priest back and got a time and an address. Father Paul added, "It's my sister's house. The girl doesn't dare go outside for fear the cult will find her."

"I'd like to bring my friend Cate Adams; she works in a psychiatric practice. Maybe she can ease the girl's concerns."

Father Paul agreed but cautioned that Em might not like it.

"Emma? Is that her name?"

"It's not Emma. It's just the letter M. It's sad, but the girls in the cult don't get names."

Sad, Cate agreed as Landry muted his phone. Tonight was for them: cocktails, music, and a great seafood meal capped by a night of quality time alone.

A noise woke Landry. He glanced at the clock on his nightstand. Four forty-three a.m. Cate was snoring beside him. He heard the noise again. Awake now, he realized it was his phone; he'd left it on mute. He looked at the screen; it was Father Paul again.

He closed the bedroom door, tiptoed to the living room, and took the call.

Usually calm and reassuring, the priest's voice was shaky now. Landry felt the apprehension as he spoke two words.

"She's gone."

"Where are you?"

"Here in New Orleans at my sister's place. I drove down last night after I spoke with you. I got here around ten thirty. Em was already asleep; my sister, Valerie, looked in on her, and everything was fine. We talked, and around midnight she went to her room, and I bedded down on the living room couch. A few minutes ago Val woke me up. There was a noise, and she got up to check. Em's bedroom door was standing wide open, and she had disappeared."

CHAPTER TWENTY-THREE

The girl wandered from one street to another, keeping out of the light and ducking around corners if someone approached. She was cold; she didn't own a coat, and the light dress Val had bought her was no match for the predawn chill. The air was heavy with moisture and she knew rain was coming soon.

She didn't know where she was or where she would go. She'd left the security of Val's home and gone into the scariest place imaginable — the outside world. Elder Johnson Lafont would be looking for her by now, and she believed he would find her. The elder had strange powers, or at least he made people think he did. Em was a believer; it wouldn't be long before Elder Johnson deduced where she was. She was a long way from New Asher and the commune didn't have cars, but that wouldn't matter. They would find a way and she would be dead. But only after they made her suffer for her sins.

Why was she here on the street instead of in the safe place Father Paul had brought her? When she'd crept out into the living room and saw him sleeping on the couch, she almost changed her mind. He was her friend. He had protected her and he had done everything he said he would. So far. But instead of turning around, she had slipped out the front door without waking him.

Em had fled because she feared talking to that man from the TV station. She had left the message in hopes someone would come to New Asher and rescue her people. Now Father Paul wanted her to meet a man, look him in the eyes, and let him inside her heart and mind. She couldn't do that.

In the short time she'd been away from the cult, she had learned that the real world was far different from her own. Everything moved fast — the way people talked and walked and drove cars, the strange computer that let you buy things today and get them tomorrow, and the stories she watched on Val's TV. It was like a million things swirling in her head at once, and her mind couldn't process it.

Every time she looked at the TV, she imagined her face there. What if she talked to the reporter and then he put her inside the TV? She knew in this crazy world it could happen, and then they would find her for sure. She was afraid to meet that man, but she didn't want to disappoint Father Paul. As frightening as it was, she left.

By seven the sun was up and the humidity made the air thick and sticky. It was over eighty degrees and she was thirsty and hot. She had no money, no shoes, no idea where to go, and no way to read the signs, because Em was illiterate, as were all the girls in the cult.

Em wandered around, unwilling to cross the street because she didn't understand the traffic signals. There was a woman in front of a house, using a garden hose to water flowers. The lady looked friendly, and because she was thirsty, Em took a chance.

"May I have a drink of water?"

The lady stared at her for a moment. "Sure, honey. Let me get you a glass."

Em shook her head and drank from the hose. It tasted wonderful, and she ran a little on her hair to cool down.

"What's wrong?" the woman asked. "Are you in trouble? Is someone bothering you?"

That scared her. She shouldn't have talked to the lady. "No. I'm okay. I need to go now." She backed away, turned and ran.

An NOPD cruiser was driving by and the lady flagged it down. She described the frail, half-dressed girl who had taken off running down Julia Street. "I can tell she's scared; she was nervous as a cat. I think someone abused her, and she ran away."

They located the girl and took her to the station. At first they thought she had mental problems. She didn't seem to know what police were. She wouldn't talk for a long time, and when a female sergeant coaxed words from her at last, she told them her name was Em and she was from New Asher. A quick search revealed no town by that name in Louisiana or its surrounding states.

When asked how old she was, she replied, "Old enough to breed," which confounded them. She couldn't answer what day or year it was, and she couldn't read or write. The girl had been staying in a house near where they picked her up, but didn't know the address. She knew just two names — a priest named Father Paul and his sister, Val, both adults. Val lived somewhere nearby, but the man lived somewhere else.

She went berserk when they said they would post her picture on the evening news. She bit, scratched, kicked and screamed, "No! No, don't put my picture on the TV! They'll kill me!"

Finally they were getting somewhere. She *was* running away from someone, probably the ones she had mentioned: Val and Father Paul.

Despite her protestations, they took her picture. The local stations ran public service ads asking for help to identify a confused girl named Em Savary who claimed to be from New Asher.

Landry saw the photo and called Father Paul. Thirty minutes later he was at the station. A relieved and exhausted Em hugged him tightly.

He explained that he and his sister were protecting her from abusive parents in Vermilion Parish and trying to get help for her. Em asked to go with him, and Father Paul gave them his driver's license. After his church in Abbeville confirmed everything, the cops handed her over.

Two hours later Junior Conreco got a call from his dispatcher. New Orleans police had called as a courtesy, advising they had released a girl named Em who said she lived in New Asher. The girl left with a priest from Abbeville named Paul Broussard. The cops wanted to make sure the parish sheriff knew about the incident.

Junior had a current link to the Sons of Jehovah for the first time. Father Paul had a girl who was from New Asher, a name too close to the old town to be coincidence. This was alarming news, and it could create serious problems.

He called the chairman of the Conclave and told him everything.

CHAPTER TWENTY-FOUR

Junior stopped at the entrance to the gated community and flashed his badge to a security guard.

"Good to see you, Sheriff. I saw your squad car coming, and I hoped there wasn't any trouble inside. Gotta keep the folks happy, you know!"

Oh yeah, Conreco knew. The rich folks paid a fortune for privacy and security, and their money allowed them deferential treatment from everyone, cops included. His blood pressure always rose when he came here. He told himself to get over it, because things would never change. The rich got richer while the rest stayed the same. Besides, tonight's meeting might be the most important ever.

He'd made this same trip three times over the past twenty years. It took an hour for him to come from Abbeville. The governor's trip was longer, but he had a chauffeur.

He drove along a tree-lined avenue for over a mile, passing mansions set far back from the road and facing Vermilion Bay. Joel Morin called his place a *cottage* — his cozy nine-thousand-square-foot lake house on the water that didn't make Junior as jealous as the man's boathouse did.

The first time the Conclave met here, Joel had given everyone a tour of the grounds. Across a broad expanse of manicured lawn sat a low-slung ranch house with a monster yacht in a slip next to it. At first he thought someone else lived there, but Joel laughed and said it was a boathouse.

Just a boathouse. It was bigger than the one Junior lived in — maybe fifteen hundred square feet — and nicer. It had two bedrooms, a full bath, outdoor shower, and a fireplace for those cool winter evenings. The boat dock adjoined it, so this wasn't even technically a boathouse, but Joel used that term because that's what rich people did.

And what sat in the slip was no boat. It was a Ferretti eighty-seven footer, Joel said as they took a tour. Five bedrooms, furniture nicer than anything Junior ever owned, and a price tag of five mil new. Junior found that out from the internet.

Joel Morin owned a timber company his great-uncle had started. While touring the boat, Junior thought about how many logs it took to buy one of those babies. A dozen more boathouses sat around the lake, each with its own big-ass boat. He burned inside; he wanted what rich people had. Why couldn't he take his family out on the lake in his five-million-dollar boat? Why? Because he made eighty-seven thousand a year, had a mortgage and bills and kids and everything else Joel Morin didn't have.

He pulled to the front of the house and parked his squad car alongside David Hebert's BMW. The governor's limousine sat idling nearby, and the driver waved to him. Joel's Bentley sat in a garage across the driveway.

Junior wondered why Joel didn't have a man park the car and another one open the door, like up at the governor's mansion. *I would,* he thought in another of his fat-cat fantasies.

He walked down a long hall to the library, where the others stood mixing drinks from a trolley. The last to arrive, he got a drink, and Joel called the meeting to order. Auguste Dauphin's chair was empty as always.

Junior wondered if Joel's anger at the funeral director had ebbed, but in a moment he heard the chairman advise why he'd called another meeting so soon. Landry Drake persisted in nosing around the parish.

"You recall that our friend David here left Landry with a challenge to learn about the mysterious goings-on in Asher. Even though we've heard nothing from the Sons of Jehovah in years, there's fresh evidence that not only are they still in existence, but our investigator Mr. Drake knows about them."

He talked about Em Savary, the girl whose picture was on TV. She lived in New Asher, and the Conclave therefore had a problem.

The governor said, "This is the most serious crisis we've faced. If the rest of you aren't upset, you should be. What do we do next, Joel?"

The cult girl's appearance complicated things. Before only Landry was their issue, but now there was a girl and a priest.

Whom should he use? He weighed each of the Conclave members in his mind. Waymon Ferrara possessed power and influence, but in his high-profile position, people would ask questions if he became involved in this situation. Not only did David Hebert have nothing to offer, Joel now believed he was even stupider than the sheriff, if that was possible.

Joel's vast wealth couldn't fix this problem. Stopping Landry and the girl required finesse and careful orchestration so things would appear normal. They must die, but making it happen without arousing suspicion would be tricky.

The last man standing, so to speak, was Junior Conreco, a man with faults. Unintelligent, brash and crude, he was also loyal and followed orders, albeit simple ones he could understand. Joel would guide him; he would be the puppeteer to Junior's Pinocchio.

Junior drove home that night weighted by a heavy burden. According to Joel, he was the only one who could fix the problem. Eliminate Landry, the priest and the girl, Joel had ordered. Get rid of them so they could never tell their secrets.

Eliminate them? Junior had asked if he meant murder, and Joel stared back in silence.

The chairman had said he would guide Junior every step of the way, but Junior saw this as his big opportunity. There had to be another way to solve the problem without killing three people, because Junior refused to do that. The Conclave had faced scares before — times when people got too close to the truth — but they'd never discussed *eliminating* people — especially a girl and a priest.

He would come up with a better solution. His ingenuity would impress the others. A lowly sheriff steps up and saves everyone's skins. That would show them.

CHAPTER TWENTY-FIVE

Four people sat around Val Broussard's kitchen table. A fifth — Landry's cameraman Phil — joined them at first, but Em flew into a tantrum, refusing to be on video. She said Landry could record her words but not her face, and he sent Phil back to the station.

Father Paul sat on one side of the girl and Val on the other, and she gripped their hands as Landry took out his notes and turned on the recorder. She did well during his questioning; she lacked formal education, but she had intelligence and keen powers of observation. She told a bizarre tale of a cult more suited for the eighteen hundreds than today.

Em slowly accepted that instead of being a threat, Landry wanted to help her like Father Paul and Val. She opened up, offering personal opinions, experiences, and taking them deep into the inner workings of life in a commune.

One important fact was that the current elder passed down oral histories to young people. This was one of the few things female children took part in, and Em had memorized many of them. She recounted the tale about the night the vigilantes burned Asher from the cult's perspective. The men who came down the river that night were drunk and crazy with rage, and they murdered several men. Even worse, they did something awful to a young girl. Em refused to discuss it; either she didn't know, or she wouldn't tell.

"The deacons caught one of them," she continued. "The others were already in their boats, and they watched the deacons hang their friend. He was the baddest of all — after what he done to that girl, he got what he deserved."

She related how the cult had moved far away to a place in dense woods near a bayou and built New Asher, where she was born and raised. Landry asked her about girls from Abbeville who had disappeared over the years, including the three whose bodies turned up.

"Guess our folks still hold a grudge," she replied without emotion.

"Are you saying the Sons of Jehovah sometimes kidnap girls and kill them?"

"No! I ain't sayin' that 'cause I don't know. I never saw anybody take girls. But maybe it happened because those men from Abbeville did some awful things that night."

"You didn't see it, but did you hear stories?"

"I don't want to talk about that anymore. You want to ask me something else?"

Landry's next question evoked a powerful reaction. A split second after he asked about Billy Whistler, her face went dark, she shook her head violently, beat her fists on the table, and screamed, "No! No!" Then she jumped up and ran from the room.

Afraid she'd leave again, Val followed her to the bathroom, but Em slammed the door and told her to go away. She left the sobbing girl alone for a few minutes before coaxing her out. She brought her back to the table and gave her a Dr Pepper, something that was her favorite thing.

He apologized for upsetting her, although he wished he could coax information out of her about Billy Whistler. He turned to another topic.

"Do you know what a rougarou is?"

She nodded her head. "That's what *he* is."

"The — the name I said a minute ago that upset you? Billy?"

Another nod, and she said she was through talking about bad things.

Lee Alard called Billy Whistler a ghoul and said some called him a rougarou. She thinks so too. Are the rougarou real?

He asked if she'd ever been to old Asher. She'd been there only once, for a Remembering Day celebration a long time ago. People from New Asher went there by wagon or on foot. He asked how long the trip took. Instead of telling him in hours — she didn't know the concept of time — she said they left after sunrise and were there by lunch. They spent the night and returned the next day. From that, he deduced that New Asher was around ten miles east of the Vermilion River.

Lee had called Remembering Day a legend, but now Landry had proof. And he was certain it fell on May 26th. It was unlikely anything was more important in the cult's history, and a "remembering" ritual made sense.

She described huge bonfires built among the foundations of long-gone buildings, and people who sat in groups and talked throughout the night. They spoke of the ones who died, and they visited graves in the cemetery that lay in the woods behind the ruined town.

He was glad she'd mentioned the cemetery.

"How many people are buried there?" Cate had thought around seventy.

"A whole lot. They still bring people there to bury 'em."

I thought so. "Even now? Why, after all these years?"

"Because Asher's so important. Elder Johnson says we can never forget what happened that night. They carry bodies over from New Asher whenever somebody dies, to let them lie beside their ancestors."

"How many people live in New Asher?"

"There's over forty families, and every family has four or five people if you include the Strange Ones."

"The strange ones?"

"The ones who aren't right, know what I mean? Like touched in the head or messed up in the body. Stuff like that."

"Are there a lot?"

"Yeah, every family's got some. They're born that way. They aren't fit for breeding, but the women take care of them. Some of them grow up and all, but they die way earlier than regular folks. Usually they behave, but sometimes one has to be put down if he gets ornery."

Landry wrote a word on his yellow pad and turned it toward Father Paul.

Inbreeding.

CHAPTER TWENTY-SIX

The Conclave wasn't the only group interested in finding Em. Elder Johnson Lafont wanted her even more than they did. She belonged to the cult, and he knew ways to deal with errant members of his flock.

One shopkeeper in Erath welcomed Elder Johnson when he and his deacons came to town for supplies. The strange men had something the merchant liked very much — ninety percent silver dollars. When he asked the elder about it once, the man shrugged it off, saying his people had accumulated a lot of the old cartwheels back in the old days when people used them as money.

Today they were worth twenty times their face value because of their rarity and silver content, but the elder spent them in the store like they were only worth a buck. The merchant made more profit on the coins than the goods they bought. The shopkeeper performed a delicate balancing act, keeping the Sons of Jehovah as customers while assuring his neighbors he wasn't aiding and abetting the devil's work.

Elder Johnson secretly used his cell phone for more than emergencies. He also sent and received text messages, although he kept that modern convenience a secret. The night Em appeared on New Orleans television, the sympathetic merchant texted Elder Johnson. His lost sheep was found, and the cult leader offered five hundred silver dollars if the man captured her.

Five hundred silver dollars converted to about $10,000! He said he'd find her, and the next morning he began his quest.

Getting information proved simple. He called the police station, identified himself as her uncle, and learned she had left with a friend, a priest from Abbeville named Paul Broussard. A lady at the church said that the cleric went to see his sister in New Orleans. He crossed his fingers that the sister was single, and sure enough, he found Valerie Broussard's listing in the online white pages. She lived off Magazine Street in the Warehouse District.

The merchant drove to New Orleans, found the house, and saw a Channel Nine news van in the driveway. It meant she was there, because he'd seen her picture on that same station. He thought they could be interviewing her; he parked down the street and walked to the house.

———

Landry had just finished interviewing Em when the doorbell rang. Val went to answer it and returned a moment later. It had been a man looking for a house, but he was on the wrong street.

Exhausted from the questions, Em went to her bedroom for a nap. Father Paul and Landry sat at the table as Val poured coffee.

"She can't stay here any longer," the priest said. "She didn't want the police to put her picture on TV, and she was right, even though we found her because of it. Now the world knows she's in New Orleans, and that means she's in danger if she stays here."

The others agreed, but no one could think of a solution. It couldn't be in Abbeville because of the issues surrounding Asher.

He had an idea. He called Cate, summarized the situation, and put her on speakerphone. He laid out the plan, and it seemed perfect. In a place far from New Orleans that no one would suspect, Em would be safe.

Cate had to put everything together. Thirty minutes later she called back to say everything had been arranged.

For now, Em and Valerie would be Callie's guests at Beau Rivage.

The merchant sat in his car a safe distance away, watching Father Paul and Landry load an SUV with suitcases and boxes. He knew the girl was there; he'd heard a young person's voice when the woman answered the door. Em Savary came out of the house with that woman. They hugged Father Paul and Landry, got in the car, and drove away.

As he pulled into traffic behind them, he considered texting Elder Johnson, but decided he'd wait until he knew their destination.

CHAPTER TWENTY-SEVEN

Callie met Val and Em on the highway at the turnoff to her B&B. They stood on the shoulder, ignoring the only other car on the road as it crept past them. Callie led them to her house and set them up in adjoining bedrooms upstairs.

When Em saw the beautiful oak trees that ringed the home and watched a boat moving down the Atchafalaya River, she fell in love with Beau Rivage. There were no other guests, and that evening as they sat on the veranda, Em relaxed. She and Val turned in early, and as she snuggled down under a thick duvet, she hoped the bad things had ended.

The man from Erath had slowed when the SUV pulled to the shoulder where a young woman waited. He drove a half mile and stopped. This part of the state was unfamiliar to him; a sign had indicated to St. Landry Parish, and a few miles back they'd passed through a little town called Krotz Springs.

After a few minutes he doubled back to find the cars gone. There was a sign: "Beau Rivage. Bed & breakfast in an antebellum mansion." An arrow pointed to a dirt road.

He crept down a one-lane road so narrow that trees on both sides brushed his car. He came to two brick pillars spanned by wrought iron with the name Arceneaux. Down a long driveway flanked by magnolias was a beautiful old house with the SUVs parked nearby.

He could go no closer for fear of being spotted, and he couldn't stay put. If another car came down the road, he'd have to go to the house to turn around.

He put the car in reverse and backed a mile to the highway. In Krotz Springs, he gassed the car and walked in the station through an ancient screen door. The man behind the counter was gruff, but he answered a few questions. The girl who owned Beau Rivage was a member of the Arceneaux family, who had built the mansion. Her name was Callie Pilantro.

Armed with that information, he texted Elder Johnson.

The girl is in hiding, but I have located her. I will bring her to you soon.

His text sounded more optimistic than the situation warranted. He had been a merchant with a predictable life. Now, enticed by ten thousand dollars, he plotted to kidnap a girl and return her to the cult she'd escaped from. The concept sounded simple, but how to do it confounded him.

Interstate 10 ran just a few miles south, and he stayed the night at the first motel he found. He slept little, worrying that he wasn't up to the challenge. Finally he thought of something that might work.

He passed through the brick gates and drove to Beau Rivage. The two cars hadn't moved; he parked beside them and went into the office.

No one was around, although there were voices somewhere in the house. He walked through another door into a spacious hallway and looked around the magnificent old house.

"Sorry, I didn't know you'd come in."

He turned to face the same attractive girl he saw on the highway yesterday.

"May I help you?"

"I'd like a room."

She apologized and said she had none at the moment.

"But the parking lot's empty."

In the hall behind her, the priest's sister walked by.

"Sorry, but I can't help you. Perhaps another time."

"I've read about your B&B, and I've come a long way. If it's not possible to stay, may I at least walk around and see the place?"

There's something not right about this. Here stood a single man who wanted to stay in her secluded bed-and-breakfast. She never had solo guests; couples and families made up her clientele.

"Where are you from?"

"Uh, Georgia. I'm just passing through on the way to California to visit family."

"I'm way off Interstate 10, and you came all the way up here just to stay at my place? How did you learn about Beau Rivage?"

He felt beads of sweat on his brow. He hadn't expected an interview. "I … I looked you up on the internet."

She stuck out her hand. "I'm Callie Pilantro."

"Nice to meet you."

"And your name is —"

He glanced around the room and noticed a filing cabinet in the corner. "Files. Uh, John Files. Nice to meet you. Do you mind if I look around after I came all this way?"

Callie was concerned. The man was lying, and she wasn't about to let him in the house with Em here. "That won't be possible, Mr. Files. Maybe another time."

She watched through the window as he got into his car and drove away. He'd said he was from Georgia, but his car had Louisiana plates. She took down the tag number and decided turning him away was a good thing.

Father Paul called and talked to Em for over an hour. When she brought the phone back to Callie, she said, "I'm going to Asher with Father Paul and Landry."

Callie wondered what Landry was thinking. Em was here for her own safety, so why would he take her back to Vermilion Parish? It made no sense.

She called Father Paul and challenged him. "How can you do this?" she asked, and he explained how he intended to keep a low profile and ensure her safety.

"She'll be back with you before anyone knows she was there," he assured Callie, and she reluctantly agreed.

CHAPTER TWENTY-EIGHT

People loved the middle of May in south Louisiana. It brought everyone outdoors. Abundant sunshine, warm temperatures, and placid lakes and rivers teeming with fish invigorated everyone. "Sportsman's paradise," Louisiana license tags declared. May was a glorious month indeed.

Landry had a busy morning taping segments for upcoming shows. When they broke for lunch, he walked to Central Grocery on Decatur next to the French Market. It was where the muffuletta sandwich originated, a New Orleans tradition that tourists and locals alike savored.

He bought a beer and crossed the street to Latrobe Park, where he found a bench in the shade to eat his lunch. On days like this he yearned to be anywhere but in a soundproofed room crammed full of equipment, with a director on the other side of a glass wall cueing him when to speak. He had an hour of taping left, and he promised himself by five he'd be sitting outdoors somewhere in the Quarter with a cocktail in his hand.

Landry fingered the vial that hung on a chain around his neck. Once things began making sense, he wondered how to protect himself. An online search revealed the solution, but it wasn't for sale anywhere.

Living in New Orleans had its advantages. Oddities of all sorts were available in this unusual city. There was a voodoo shop on Bourbon Street where a man who called himself Zombie sold souvenirs to tourists. But a few months ago while exploring the French Quarter one Saturday afternoon, Landry had found the real thing. A faded wooden sign reading "Potions and such" hung from a dilapidated picket fence on Dumaine Street. He rang the bell that day, and an old black man answered the door, looked him up and down, and said, "You don't need nothin'. Don't come back 'til you does."

He had left, but later he came back, stood on the porch, and rang the bell again. Lace curtains parted and a pair of eyes stared at him. The curtains closed and the same man opened the door. He invited Landry into the strangest front room he'd ever seen. *Only in the French Quarter.* The room looked like a store, lined with shelves and tables packed with jars, vials and envelopes. On a table were a mortar and pestle and a scale.

Embarrassed to say what he wanted, Landry said he wanted a joke for a friend.

"It ain't for no friend," the old man said. "It's for you, and you're gonna need it." From a dusty shelf he pulled an old glass jar filled with what looked like dried purple flowers. Using the mortar, he crushed them into tiny pieces and poured them into a glass vial with a stopper on one end and a metal plunger on the other. The ampule hung on a thin silver chain.

"Wear it around your neck," the man said. "When you're ready to use it, you presses the button here. Aim it where it's needed and them flowers fly out and do the trick."

As Landry put the chain around his neck, he asked himself what the hell he was doing. "Are you sure this stuff works?"

"For a hunnerd bucks it ought to." The old man laughed.

The strangest part of the odd visit happened when he left, and the old proprietor walked with him out to the porch. As Landry reached the gate, he said, "Your secret's safe with me, Mr. Landry." Then he turned and went back inside.

He decided not to mention his purchase to Cate. She'd think him crazy or scared, and it was a subject best left alone. But if something bad happened, the flowers might save his life. If they worked at all. Like Lee Alard said, lots of things were just tales.

Landry finished lunch and returned to the studio to finish the taping. Back in his office later, he listened to a voicemail from Father Paul. No problems, the priest had said, but call when you can. He was glad his friend had added the preface; he had checked in with Callie just that morning and all was well at Beau Rivage. Regardless, this was no time to relax because Elder Johnson would still be looking for her.

Father Paul and Landry had discussed asking Em to go to Asher with them. She'd been there and her observations might help. Her safety was their biggest concern, but if they kept everything quiet, they would be in and out of Asher undetected.

The priest had good news. He'd talked at length with Em today. Although apprehensive, she agreed to go to Asher.

"That's great! But how will we get there? Clearly we can't use Catfish again."

"For her safety, we'll stay away from Abbeville and Perry entirely. We won't go downriver this time; we'll come up from the south. One of my parishioners lives down on Bayou Vermilion. He's a crawfish farmer, and he uses an airboat to run his traps. I spoke to him right before I called you. He'll take us to Asher."

"How much did you have to tell him?"

"Nothing. I said a friend wanted to visit a ghost town. He's a man of few words and even fewer questions."

"How can you be sure he won't talk?"

"He and his dog live in a house on the bayou south of Esther, and he sells live crawfish to the c-store over in Henry. He's reclusive, so there's no one for him to tell if he knew anything. My only concern is if he recognizes you. Even people in the sticks have TVs. Your being along might mean we have to come up with a few more answers, but we can deal with that when the time comes."

Landry wanted to go as soon as possible, but Father Paul cautioned against moving too fast. "It took a lot of patient coaxing to get her to this point. If it appears we're in a hurry and she gets nervous, she might back off. We'll say that we appreciate her help, but not make it a big deal."

Landry left it in the priest's hands and said he was ready anytime, and the next Saturday, Father Paul met Val and Em in Lafayette. Em jumped in his car and they headed off. The plan was he'd call Val in the late afternoon and bring Em back to the same spot.

Landry followed the priest's directions and drove north on highway 333. At Bayou Road near Esther he turned east toward the river. He came to a house. Father Paul and Em stood in the yard, and nearby a man sat in an airboat, tinkering with its motor.

Father Paul's description of the old guy had been spot on. The rare times he talked, he stared at the ground and mumbled. He was painfully antisocial, and at last Father Paul put him out of his misery and boarded the boat for their trip. The noise from the huge fan would keep talk to a minimum, which suited the old fellow.

The Erath merchant watched helplessly as the airboat pulled away from shore. Once they boarded the airboat, his hours of trailing them were over. He had no way to follow them further.

He texted Elder Johnson and told him where he was and what had happened. The man also requested partial payment because he had diligently followed them. He returned to Erath and waited for a response that never came.

Em and Landry sat in the middle of the boat and Father Paul rode in the bow. As the huge fan in the back began to propel them north, she asked Landry if he knew who Jesus was. He chuckled but stopped when he realized she meant it.

"Sure. Pretty much everybody knows who Jesus is."

"I never heard of him until Father Paul told me. For us, Elder Johnson was kind of our Jesus. At least that's what him and the deacons wanted people to think. But they're wrong about that. Father Paul says a man can't be god, and people shouldn't worship a man. What do you think?"

Landry nodded, and she said the reason she agreed to go to Asher was because Father Paul helped her understand that Elder Johnson and his men treated people — especially women — badly. He had told Em that if she took Landry to Asher and explained about it, perhaps Landry could help other cult members.

She changed the subject. "Jesus loves the little children, and he says men and women are all the same," she declared. "God named everything, even the fish and bugs, and Father Paul said my new name is Emily. Em for short!" She grinned and her enthusiasm about the priest and her new friend Jesus made him smile too.

In a few minutes the fisherman headed towards the bank. Landry looked for other boats, but everything was quiet.

The most important thing on today's agenda was taking Em to the cemetery. He wanted to ask about people still being buried there. They left the old man with the boat, went through the town, and walked through the woods to the graveyard.

She pointed out a mound of dirt with a flat stone on it. "This one's from the last Remembering Day. Deacon Philip's wife R died. They brought her body over in a wagon and they buried her during the night while everyone celebrated. That was when I came for Remembering Day, and I saw the whole thing."

The stone had crude etchings — a letter *R* and the year 2010. It was a sad memorial to the life of a person who wasn't even allowed a name just because she was a woman. And the date confirmed that Remembering Day happened every ten years. The next one was less than a year away.

He showed her the Savary graves he'd found last time, with the dates 2007 and 2009. "I knew them," she said. "K Savary was a Strange One." Landry recalled her words. *Every family has one or two. They're born that way — they're not right.*

Landry noticed something he'd missed earlier. Most graves lay undisturbed, the dirt smooth and rounded. This one was disrupted, its sod tossed here and there. A sunken depression lay where a body should be.

"Why does this grave look so different?"

Em stared at it but didn't answer.

Father Paul whispered, "Em, whose grave is that?"

"A Strange One."

"How can you tell?"

"Because the dirt's all messed up."

"What does that mean?"

"It means they ain't there. When they bury them, sometimes they ain't quite dead."

Father Paul and Landry glanced at each other in astonishment while Em strolled through other graves.

Landry opened his mouth to speak, but the priest put a hand on his arm. They had to be careful with her.

"Em, what are you talking about?"

"Sometimes they go into a state like being dead, but not exactly. They can be that way for days. After a while Elder Johnson decides they died and orders the deacons to bury 'em."

She knelt at the head of the disturbed grave and brushed dirt off the stone. When she looked at the inscription, she bounded up and almost fell.

"What did you find?"

"Nothing." That was a lie; her hands were shaking. She hugged herself so the men wouldn't notice.

Landry looked at the chiseled marks — *BW 1883* — and pointed them out to the priest.

"1883. That's an old one," Father Paul said.

Anxious now, Em moved toward the path they'd come down. "Take me back. This place scares me."

Landry didn't understand about this grave, but he could tell something was significant by the way she acted. He asked if she remembered the person, and she nodded.

"Were you here when they buried him?"

"No. That was a long time ago."

"Then how do you remember him?"

The hair rose on his arms when she answered, "Because he's still around. I seen him."

Landry noticed she had become agitated. "Please help me understand. Tell me how you can see a dead person."

She grimaced. "'Cause it's him! It's Billy Whistler! I don't want to tell you anything more. You're scaring me. You shouldn't have made me come here!" She ran down the path into the forest and was out of sight in seconds.

Father Paul called after her. "Em! Wait, Em! We'll take you back right now. Don't worry!"

They ran down the trail to the shore, where the old man sat in his boat, whittling on a stick with a pocketknife.

Father Paul yelled, "Did the girl come out a minute ago?"

He shook his head. "Ain't nobody come out of the woods except you two."

It had taken only a few minutes to run down the trail from the graveyard, so she couldn't have gone far. They retraced their steps along the path, calling her name and pausing to listen, and they looked for signs of disturbance to indicate where she might have gone off into the woods. In minutes, she had vanished.

Landry felt responsible. She hadn't wanted to come, but for his own selfish motives — to learn more about the cult — she might be in danger.

Wherever she was, one thing was certain. Her life was worth nothing if the cult got her back. They had to move quickly.

CHAPTER TWENTY-NINE

Hysterical, Em ran along the narrow trail. She wanted to be far, far away from that graveyard. She would wait for Landry and Father Paul at the boat and make them take her back.

Em gasped for breath as the trees seemed to close in around her. She tripped on a root and fell face-first on the hard-packed dirt. There was a smell — something pungent, nasty and familiar.

A bony hand reached from the underbrush next to her and clapped itself over her mouth, stifling her scream. Another hand wrapped around her ankle and dragged her off the trail into the bushes seconds before Landry and Father Paul passed only two feet from them.

The creature listened to their voices. They were at the river, but they'd return soon to search for the girl. She had fainted, which pleased him. Otherwise he would have shut her up himself. He crept out onto the path, swept away the drag marks, crawled back into the bushes and arranged them so no one would notice.

He stood with his back hunched and his apelike arms almost dragging on the ground. He easily lifted her limp body and carried her deep into the woods to the safe place.

He'd watched the whole time. He'd heard the airboat approaching, and he saw the three of them walk through Asher to the grave place. Without the power of deductive reasoning, he had only basic thoughts involving immediate wants or needs, but he remembered the girl. She was one of them. She had been afraid of him once, like all of them, and he was afraid of her too. He understood cause and effect: when his kind approached the others, the tall man would beat them. He had steered clear of her back at New Asher, but now she belonged to him.

His eyes had gleamed when he'd watched her kneel to examine that one grave — his grave — and look at the stone. He didn't know what it said, but when she ran away, he snatched her, and that pleased him. He possessed a clever instinct for survival, and he could hide things from the others — the ones who hated his kind — but now there was something special to hide. He'd caught one of them. His conquest made him salivate with pleasure, even though he had no idea what he was going to do with her. He was asexual, so he considered Em a prize he'd won. He couldn't talk to her because his communication skills were almost nonexistent. He could speak perhaps twenty words in his guttural rasp. He wanted to look at her and touch her arm for now. He would kill her later.

He sat blocking the entrance to the little cave and whistled as he watched her. Had he killed her? He hoped not. When she stirred at last, he gave her a grimacing, toothless smile. She opened her eyes wide, saw the thing sitting in front of her with its high, sloping forehead and wispy hair, and she realized what it was. She screamed and screamed until she passed out again, her brain drifting into merciful darkness.

The cave muffled her screams and so the searchers a half mile away heard nothing.

———

What had been a boat trip to Asher was now the search for a missing girl, and it was time to notify the authorities. Since they were in Vermilion Parish, they should call the sheriff, but Landry thought Junior wouldn't help him, even to save a life.

Calling the state police was his only other choice. Landry knew a lieutenant named Harry Kanter, with whom he had worked on another case. He got his friend on the line, and Kanter asked why he didn't call the sheriff. Landry explained, but it didn't work.

Kanter said he couldn't help unless Sheriff Conreco asked for it. "It's his baby and there's no way to keep him off it. If you've done nothing wrong, he can't order you out of his parish or lock you up. He's an officer like I am, sworn to uphold the law. Trust me on this one. There's no way around it, and you're wasting valuable time talking to me when you should already be on the horn to him."

Father Paul was the one who called. He explained what had happened and who was missing without mentioning Landry's name. The dispatcher took his number and location, promising to send help as soon as possible. They hoped it wouldn't be Junior.

What Landry and Father Paul didn't realize was that the sheriff had to come. There was too much at stake and they were getting close.

They heard an outboard motor before the boat rounded the bend. The sheriff's face looked grim as he steered the craft to shore and secured it next to the airboat, where the old crawfish farmer still sat whittling. Conreco and a deputy got out and walked to where Landry and Father Paul stood.

Junior didn't seem surprised to see him, but he spoke only to the priest, as if Landry didn't exist. Father Paul explained why they came. They'd brought a girl to Asher who had escaped from the cult, hoping she could enlighten them about the graves. He told the sheriff what they had been doing when she got spooked and ran.

"What's your theory?" Conreco asked. "You said something on a grave made her upset. Did she run off and hide somewhere, waiting for you to leave?"

Landry said that wasn't it, and the sheriff's glare revealed the rage inside him.

"You shut your mouth, Mr. Drake. Don't say a word. No high-powered lawyer's going to claim I made you talk without counsel present. I'm playing this one by the books. And we might as well get to it. Deputy, cuff Mr. Drake here and read him his rights."

"What are you doing?" Father Paul asked. "He hasn't done anything —"

"Be careful, Father. Your words may be used against you too. Maybe you didn't realize what he was up to, scheming to make up stories about Asher to put on his big TV show. He's snuck around this parish long enough. I warned him. I warned both of you that day at the RiverFront. I let him off the other times, even when he stole a boat, but now I've got him dead to rights!" The sheriff folded his arms and threw a satisfied smirk Landry's way.

Landry stood with his hands cuffed in back. "What the hell are you talking about? What have I done?"

"Kidnapping, for starters. A girl runs off and two grown men can't find her five minutes later? Bullshit, gentlemen. If we find the girl dead, things are gonna go very badly for you. Possibly you too, Father. Make this easier for me and I might recommend leniency. Why don't you just tell me what really happened? Little hanky-panky in the woods? Something like that? Little fun with a young one? I don't blame you for that, but what happened then? Did things get out of hand?"

He looked sympathetically at the priest. "Father, I'm hoping none of this involves you. If he brought you and the girl here and started doing bad things, tell me and you're off the hook. I just want the facts."

"The facts?" Landry yelled. "You haven't said anything factual yet. Why aren't we out looking for the girl?"

"Great idea, Mr. Drake. Why don't you tell us where to begin?"

CHAPTER THIRTY

Harry Kanter wondered how things had ended with Landry. He searched the web for information about a missing female, but instead he found a sensational story. The well-known Louisiana ghost hunter Landry Drake was in the Vermilion Parish jail for kidnapping.

Kanter was acquainted with Junior Conreco; he'd had a few cases in Vermilion Parish and found him to be a reasonable guy — not the sharpest pencil but not a bad cop. He didn't think Landry would be involved in a crime like this, but if Conreco locked him up, there had to be something there.

Curious about a man he thought he knew, Kanter called the sheriff. He said that he'd worked with Landry and it surprised him to learn he'd been arrested.

The sheriff said Landry had a dark side. The public saw him as a young investigator who enthralled people with his TV shows. Behind the facade lurked a psychopath, a molester or even a killer, but definitely a kidnapper.

"Whatever happened down at Asher, he was involved," Junior confided to his fellow lawman. "We didn't find where he put the body, but some high-powered lawyer from

New Orleans is here talking to him now. I'm hoping he'll convince his client to make it easy on everybody and come clean. He can lead us to the corpse and we'll wrap things up."

"Do you have a team combing the area where she disappeared?"

"No need, in my opinion. I'm letting my theory play out first."

"Sheriff, you're making a huge mistake. You've already convicted the man who got you involved in the first place, and no one is looking for a girl who may still be alive."

"You see it one way; I see it another. You aren't down here in the trenches."

No, but I will be soon, Kanter decided as he hung up. He went to his boss, explained the situation, and got approval.

State police Troop I in Lafayette covered Vermilion Parish. Kanter called the commander there to explain what he wanted to do. The captain said he'd send a man to Abbeville to await Kanter's arrival from Baton Rouge.

Two hours later the two state cops walked into the sheriff's office in Abbeville. Junior had stepped out, and the dispatcher called him. Kanter asked to talk with Landry Drake while they waited, and the deputy complied without question. The state cops surrendered their weapons and met Landry in a small room while the deputy stood behind them near the door.

They conversed quietly. Landry had been a friend, but his years of service taught him that some people were chameleons. Landry seemed glad he had come, and Kanter said Junior's attitude about the case puzzled him.

"Kidnapping is a crime where we offer our help to the local guys, so here I am. I have to say I never thought it'd be you on the other side of the table."

Landry smiled ruefully; it had never crossed his mind either.

Just then the door burst open, swinging so hard it hit the deputy in the face. Junior stormed in, just as furious as he'd been on the Asher shoreline when he arrested Landry.

"Get the hell out of here, Kanter! I didn't call the state for help, and you're interfering with an ongoing investigation."

"I was just explaining to Mr. Drake why I'm here. We assist local authorities on kidnappings. Let's go to your office and talk."

The sheriff fumbled his words. "Maybe it wasn't a kidnapping. It's still early in the investigation."

Kanter stood. "You called him a kidnapper. I'd prefer not to talk further in front of your prisoner. Let's go, Sheriff." He moved toward the door.

"Goddammit," Junior muttered. He pointed a finger at Landry. "Before this is over, you're gonna be sorry you ever set foot in Vermilion Parish."

Late that afternoon Lieutenant Kanter and a deputy joined Sheriff Conreco and four of his men to search the area where the girl had disappeared. Kanter had insisted Father Paul come too, since he had witnessed the events.

Kanter wondered what issues Junior had with Landry. For some reason, his mere presence infuriated the sheriff so much that he'd jailed him on what might be a trumped-up charge while his presumed accomplice the priest was free. If Father Paul had been present when a crime was committed, why didn't Junior detain him until things were sorted out?

They planned to search until dusk and return to Abbeville before dark. Things were wrapping up when a deputy shouted, "Over here! I found her!"

The officer had searched atop an earthen ridge next to a grove of trees. He called out the girl's name and saw something crouching in the bushes. Startled, it ran away through the trees. Seeing more movement in the tall grass, the cop aimed his weapon at a dirty, disheveled girl who crawled out of a hole in the ridge. As surprised as he, the girl ran to him and cried for help.

Father Paul ran to her, and she collapsed into his arms, safe at last. Em exonerated both Landry and the priest, and the lawmen searched for the person until dark.

"A man got me," she told Junior and Lieutenant Kanter. "I shouldn't have run away, and he caught me and dragged me into the bushes. If you all hadn't come, I don't know what he would have done."

The sheriff said, "Let's get you back to town. I need to get a statement, and then you can go home."

Back in Abbeville, the sheriff seated everyone in his conference room and asked a clerk to come in and record the girl's statement.

"Aren't you forgetting something?" Kanter said, pointing to the jail cells toward the back. "You're holding an innocent man back there. You need to cut him loose now."

Junior released Landry, who walked to where the others had gathered. As he pulled out a chair, the sheriff said, "Oh no you don't. Get the hell out of my parish and don't you ever come back."

That was the last straw for Lieutenant Kanter, and he scolded the sheriff like a child in front of everyone. "Dammit, Junior, Landry has every right to be here. Just because you don't like him nosing around, as you call it, doesn't mean he can't do it. You wasted a lot of time today on some issue between you two instead of looking for this girl. What if he'd killed her? That murder would have been on you. Keep your mind on business from now on."

Contrite, Junior mumbled that he should have handled things differently, and walked away from the others.

Em gave a brief statement and said she wanted to go to bed. Father Paul's and Landry's cars were at the crawfish farmer's house, and Lieutenant Kanter offered to drop them off. Once they were in his squad car, they asked if he could take them to Beau Rivage instead. Em needed to sleep; they'd spend the night and pick up the vehicles tomorrow.

Father Paul called his sister. She'd been waiting for news, and she wept and thanked God Em was safe. She said she would have Em's bed turned down and ready when they arrived.

Landry called Cate, who was happy for Em and pleased that at last perhaps he could work in the parish without harassment. He advised he would spend the night with the others at Callie's and check in tomorrow.

Kanter asked what the beef was between Landry and the sheriff. Landry truly didn't know, but he said the local funeral director had also demanded he get out. Junior had also told two others — a court clerk and a boat guide — to stop helping Landry.

"There's something they're trying to keep under wraps," Landry suggested, and Kanter agreed it sure looked like it. The lieutenant warned him to be careful. He knew from experience Landry wouldn't let this go, and he also believed there was more trouble for him ahead if he didn't.

Junior couldn't get to sleep that night. Everything was weighing him down. He wasn't being fair to Landry Drake. The guy was on a mission and he was putting the pieces together. Who cared if the Conclave got blown out of the water? The secrets were becoming more than he wanted to bear. He was tired of hiding things and tired of hounding Landry for no reason at all.

CHAPTER THIRTY-ONE

Tucked in bed at Beau Rivage, Em's mind somehow blocked the terror she'd experienced and gave her nine hours of sleep. She came downstairs at nine, energized after a good night's sleep and a hot shower. In her white shirt, shorts and running shoes, Father Paul thought she looked like an all-American girl — a far cry from when he first saw her in the confessional.

She joined Callie, Father Paul and Landry at the breakfast table and announced she had something to tell them. Her statement to the sheriff last night was that the graveyard had scared her and she ran away. A smelly man who walked with a stoop captured her and took her to a cave. He didn't do anything to her, nor did he speak. He just looked at her. She slept off and on, and each time she awoke he was still there, blocking the cave entrance. Much later she heard voices — men calling her name — and the man ran off just before the deputy found her.

"That isn't the real story," she revealed. "I didn't want to tell them strangers, but now I can tell you. Billy Whistler took me. He stunk like crazy and he put his nasty hand over my mouth. I got scared and passed out. I thought he wanted to kill me, but he stuck me in that little cave and watched me. I was terrified and finally someone came and he ran off. I lied about him before, but I had to tell you because he'll keep trying to get me. They sent him. Please help me."

Landry asked if she was talking about the elder, and she nodded. He would do anything to bring her back. People couldn't even discuss leaving, yet she had done it. Had the cult leader sent Billy Whistler? Did he control the creature?

"Would they hurt you if you returned to New Asher?"

She nodded. "He'd punish me first, and then he'd kill me to show the others what happens to folks who don't obey. I've seen what he does."

"We can protect you, but only if you let us," Father Paul said. "No more running away. We're here to help. You must believe us."

She wiped away her tears and nodded.

Landry asked her about the grave marker with the inscription BW 1883. "That's Billy Whistler's grave, isn't it? The dirt looked different because a Strange One was buried there who hadn't died. Then you saw the marker and ran away. But if you can't read, how did you understand what was on the marker?"

"'Cause I know what a *B* and a *W* look like. I seen them before and they mean Billy Whistler."

"So it wasn't a Strange One's grave. It was his."

"You don't understand. He *is* a Strange One. There's lots of 'em, like I told you. Billy Whistler's all bent and his brain don't work right. He's a Strange One, but he's different. Most of the Strange Ones don't live very long 'cause something's bad wrong with them, but he's lived a long time."

Landry asked if she'd heard the story of Billy Whistler and how it all began.

"Sure. Kids learn the story when they're little. He's scary and awful, but he's kind of a hero too. It's about that night when the bad men burned our town. They was drunk and they killed seven of our people. One of those guys did bad things to a girl. He poked out her eyes and made her have a baby later on. When they all ran away to their boats, our men caught the one who done the things to the girl and hanged him. A Strange One whistled and danced around while the body hung from a tree branch. After that night our folks called the Strange One Billy Whistler 'cause of his whistling. He died in 1883, but like I told you, he didn't, 'cause they buried him in that grave and he dug himself out. He's been around ever since."

"Where is he today?"

"He hides out somewhere, maybe in that cave where he took me. He does whatever he wants, I guess, but his big job comes on Remembering Day. Billy Whistler gets to catch a girl and poke her eyes out. Then he kills her. That's our special remembering for what those men did to us."

"Have you ... did you see that happen yourself?"

"Yes," she answered casually. "I went to that one Remembering Day when I was a little kid. That's when I saw it."

Her revelations stunned them all. Father Paul's eyes were closed and his lips moved imperceptibly as he uttered a prayer for the victims. When he finished, he raised his head and said to Landry, "Now we understand why girls from Abbeville have disappeared over the years." He asked Em what happened to the girls' bodies, and she said Elder Johnson left a few as a reminder of what a bad thing people had done. She couldn't answer about the others.

Out of fourteen, three bodies had been found on the riverbank. They were the girls from 1930, 1950 and 2000 — the three Landry had researched at the courthouse.

Landry felt sorry for Em. She had been raped herself, not by a twisted being called Billy Whistler but by a respected member of the cult who sought to impregnate her. When it didn't work, a second man tried it, with the same results. Those humiliating, degrading acts were so routine to the Sons of Jehovah that she had mentioned them only to explain why she fled the commune. A barren woman was a liability, and she knew her fate if she stayed.

Innocent girls were kidnapped and murdered, and Em seemed to accept the brutality as normal acts of a society. Elder Johnson was a sadistic monster, and Landry hoped they weren't too late to save Em's mind from the things she had endured.

Father Paul took her hand in his. "Em, what you've seen in your short life is horrifying. Jesus doesn't want people to hurt each other, and what Elder Johnson has done to your people is a sin. You did a good thing running away, and if I can help it, you'll never have to face those people again."

CHAPTER THIRTY-TWO

The situation in Vermilion Parish was getting out of control, and Landry had to get help. He faced a labyrinth of problems. Em had revealed unbelievable atrocities. Some people went to great lengths to keep secrets, and an ever-growing chance existed that the Sons of Jehovah would capture the girl

He saw the story — a massive cover-up that began a hundred and forty years ago — but he couldn't juggle all its parts. He called his boss and asked for a meeting.

Landry liked Ted, and not only because he was one of Landry's biggest supporters. The station manager was forty, single, and always struggling with his weight. Ted saw Landry's life as filled with adventure, and his own as dull and routine. When Landry worked on something exciting, Ted yearned to go out in the field with his ghost hunter. It would never happen, because running a metropolitan TV station, especially one with Landry Drake on the team, left no time for day trips to haunted houses in sleepy Acadian towns. Instead, he lived vicariously through the tales Landry spun about his adventures.

They met in the conference room and Landry laid out what Em had disclosed. This investigation was headed in a new and potentially dangerous direction because the Sons of Jehovah were neither extinct nor dormant. If Em's story was true, they still did the same awful tricks they'd been doing for decades.

Landry made a request that caught Ted by surprise, and he took it up the corporate ladder. He sent a summary of Landry's investigation to his boss in Chattanooga. Like everything Landry did, the request was bizarre but also exciting, and Ted hoped they'd approve it.

He wanted to know something simple. Who occupied the graves in the Asher cemetery? The Sons of Jehovah owned the private graveyard, and no records existed in the parish courthouse. He couldn't just dig the bodies up, so he approached it a different way. Landry would seek a court order to disinter the bodies. Maybe they were the missing Abbeville girls, or disfigured "Strange Ones," or others the cult leaders killed when they no longer served a purpose. There was only one way to find out.

The suits in Chattanooga liked the idea and said what Landry wanted would boost ratings. Even if they didn't get the court order, just going through the motions would generate huge publicity. Channel Nine would run clips on the story as it unfolded — the legal process in Vermilion Parish, the attempt to contact the owners of the cemetery, the cult's background and so forth — and it would generate interest even if a *Bayou Hauntings* segment never happened.

The company's general counsel told Ted to use local counsel and ensure Landry didn't break the law. He had been to the site twice, and he'd trespassed on private property. No more of that, the company's attorney cautioned, or the reporter might end up in jail for real.

Ted called the New Orleans attorney and told him about the cemetery near Asher that the Sons of Jehovah owned.

He wanted to know what steps to take to exhume bodies there.

The paralegal assigned to the project found the request curious, but he wasn't surprised. He'd seen Landry Drake's shows, and this matter — digging up bodies in an old cemetery — had to be something the investigator was working on.

Most of the time, however, his curiosity went unsatisfied. He'd do the research, submit a report, and never hear anything, because the story never got aired. He didn't waste his time wondering what Landry wanted with bodies in an ancient graveyard. Once he started, the research didn't take long. The law was well established, with plenty of precedent and clearly defined rules to request an exhumation. He gathered the information, a senior partner signed off, and Landry had the research and a legal opinion the next day.

Channel Nine's lawyers prepared a brief requesting disinterment on behalf of M Savary and other girls in the cult. The reason was to find out if murders were being committed every ten years as part of a ritual called Remembering Day.

For obvious reasons, Landry hoped to keep the sheriff out of the process. They would submit their request to the district attorney serving Vermilion Parish or to the state attorney general. If one of them chose to, he would ask a judge for an order. If the judge agreed, the exhumations would happen. If not, Channel Nine had the right to appeal.

When Landry explained his problems in Abbeville, the lawyers agreed with him that they'd submit to the state first. They would deal with parish officials only if it came to that.

News travelled fast. Five hours after they filed the brief, the NBC affiliate in Baton Rouge broke the news that a New Orleans TV station sought to open caskets in a ghost town called Asher. The newscaster linked Landry to the story as they ran file footage showing the foundations of Asher's long-gone buildings.

That this story featured a rival station was immaterial; this was a sensational human-interest piece. What was the ghost hunter working on this time? Vigilantes had murdered several men and torched the town in 1880 — were the graves of the long-dead going to give up secrets at last? Was the legend about werewolves — the rougarou — true? What about Mollie Manning, the girl whose mutilated body was found at Asher in 2010?

Landry and Ted welcomed the leak because it was great publicity for Channel Nine and the *Bayou Hauntings* series. If the matter came before a judge, the request would become public information. Attorneys would even try to find the current representative of the owner, SOJ Land Company. The cult might find out what Landry was up to, but it didn't matter. It was a decision a judge would make if things went well.

The first step didn't go as Landry had hoped. Calling the matter a parish issue, the state AG declined to consider it. Next the lawyers delivered the request to the district attorney for Acadia, Lafayette and Vermilion Parishes. Landry wasn't worried about being treated fairly; the DA was known to be an honest, decent man. But Junior Conreco seemed hell-bent on Landry's downfall. Would he try to influence the district attorney?

Soon after the sheriff saw the news report, he got a call from Joel Morin that ticked him off. It seemed to Junior that the richer people got, the less tact they had with people who weren't like themselves.

"Nip this Landry Drake thing in the bud," the leader of the Conclave had snapped. "Go to the DA, tell him this is a frivolous request by a man making a TV show, and make sure it goes no further."

How stupid are you? Junior wondered as he listened to Joel rant. The DA would say he was interfering. No matter that Joel knew nothing about how politics and justice worked in the parish. He could order other people around, but there was only one sheriff here, and Junior would handle things his own way.

And there was that nagging doubt he was having more and more often now, that niggling thing in his mind that said Landry had every right to know more.

CHAPTER THIRTY-THREE

The two parish officials sat at a corner table in The French Press across from the park in downtown Lafayette. The district attorney was a man in his fifties and spent his career as a prosecutor. He'd won his last election by a wide margin and had an excellent conviction rate. The criminals didn't think much of him, but most of the law-abiding citizenry supported him.

Thinking a face-to-face meeting was best, Junior had arranged the meeting and made the half-hour drive from Abbeville that morning. Over bacon, eggs and grits, they chatted about Vermilion Parish's improving crime rate and how well things were going overall. Then the DA apologized for his busy morning and asked what Junior wanted to talk about.

Far less eloquent and educated than the DA, Junior had practiced his speech to ensure he didn't miss anything. He explained that Landry Drake had trespassed on private land several times. He ignored orders to leave the parish, and now he was trying to get graves opened. He must be stopped, Junior said, and you can do it.

After Junior made his case, the DA said he didn't see the problem. What issues was the investigative reporter creating? Who ordered him to leave and why, and why did Junior want to stop the exhumations?

"I just don't get it, Sheriff. There's no downside to this request. I hear the landowners — the members of some cult — have been gone for ages. The brief says there are recent burials at Asher, but no one knows who they are or who buried them. The request sounds reasonable to me. Open up the graves, see if there's been foul play, and perhaps learn some answers. Convince me why I shouldn't ask a judge to grant it."

Dammit, the DA was right, and the only reason Junior had come was because Joel ordered it. He had no convincing argument, only the truth, and revealing that would have meant the end of Junior's career in law enforcement. The massive cover-up had begun a hundred and forty years ago, and the secrets in those graves would blow things wide open.

Junior tried again. "Having our parish featured that way on a TV show isn't good for us."

"What way, Junior? Is there something about the graves you aren't telling me?"

"No. Nothing at all, as far as I'm concerned. Who cares about Asher anyway? Been gone over a hundred years, right?" He caught himself talking too fast, and he paused for a breath. "No, everything's good. I just don't want our sleepy little town all filled up with amateur ghost hunters. I hear that's what happens every time Landry Drake does a story."

The DA smiled and said, "Did you see that *Bayou Hauntings* show about the abandoned insane asylum over in Iberia Parish? That was a good one, and it took place in a ghost town called Victory. Remember the show? I don't think the ghost hunters are flocking to see the ruins of that place, any more than I think exhuming the bodies would cause tourists to descend upon Asher.

"I get your idea about not wanting to create a fuss for no reason, but I have to admit that after reading Mr. Drake's brief, I'm interested myself. I'd like to learn more about the old cemetery in Asher just like he would. I'm hoping he does an episode on our parish." He looked at his watch. "I have to run. Is there anything else?"

As he drove back to Abbeville, Junior wondered what to do next. He'd blown this assignment, but if he was lucky, the judge would deny the request. If he didn't, then Junior must stop Landry himself.

The judge was inclined to allow the exhumations, but no one had heard from the landowners in years. Landry explained about Em, who said they lived in New Asher, but no one knew where it was. Em had run away but didn't know how to get back. Landry might have been able to find the cult if he tried, but he had no incentive to do so. If Elder Johnson found out, he'd oppose the request.

The judge ruled that public notices would run in newspapers in Vermilion and surrounding parishes for a week. The notices were printed, and no one appeared on behalf of the landowner.

Two weeks later the judge granted the motion, stipulating that they must complete the exhumations and reburials in thirty days. Time would be precious since no one knew how many graves there were, but Landry had anticipated a win, and he was ready to go immediately.

At daybreak on the morning after the judge's ruling, a light barge went downriver to Asher and offloaded the parish medical examiner, six laborers and a foreman, hand tools, folding tables and chairs, and large coolers with food and beverages they'd bring back and forth each day.

Landry and his cameraman Phil Vandegriff, who'd been a part of other *Bayou Hauntings* episodes, hired the crawfish farmer to bring them and their equipment up on the airboat. Ted Carpenter came along too. This all began with the voicemail, and Ted was excited to see Landry in the field for the first time.

One last boat pulled in, this one carrying Father Paul and Em. Another friend of the priest's, a guide who lived in Bancker Grotto, had picked them up in Perry and brought them to Asher.

Once everyone arrived and Phil's equipment was set up, Landry met with the diggers. He laid out the plans while Phil shot video. He would film everything since no one was sure what to expect. If a story developed, there'd be plenty of editing once the deadline passed.

Just before work started at eight, Junior Conreco and a deputy strode into the clearing. He announced that one of his men would be on site every day while Landry and his crew exhumed the bodies. Landry said he'd give the deputy the next day's schedule every evening before they left. That concession cost him nothing, and if it placated the sheriff, so much the better.

And, he thought to himself, the sheriff seemed less arrogant and dictatorial this morning. It would be nice if it lasted, but he doubted it would.

They spent the first morning mapping and plotting. After marking what they believed were the boundaries of the cemetery, they used stakes and strings to create a grid of forty-nine four-by-four-foot squares, some of which contained graves, and some that did not. In all, there were seven horizontal rows of seven squares each.

Landry drew squares on a piece of butcher paper that matched the grid. They would number and record each grave and what it contained. He told the crew to begin at one corner and work down a row before moving to the next. Landry reminded them to be careful with the digging, because these were human beings who deserved respect and a proper reburial. Not only was that part of the judge's order, it was the decent thing to do.

At noon the crew broke for lunch. Em and the priest handled food prep and set up tables and chairs near the shoreline. Everyone dug into po'boy sandwiches, fried chicken, potato salad, coleslaw, and bottles of soda and water. The two-man barge crew and the boatmen joined them, and Phil's camera caught the camaraderie as everyone ate, talked with their mouths full, and joked with each other. Even the deputy joined in; he knew most of the workers and chatted with them. The men jostled each other to get more food until what had seemed an abundance was gone.

Next came a thirty-minute siesta. Everyone lounged in the shade of huge oak trees. Some smoked cigarettes or cigars or chewed tobacco. Others found the buzzing of insects and the light breeze blowing off the river too tempting to resist, and they fell asleep.

After their break, the real work began. Landry was most interested in the disturbed grave Em had said was Billy Whistler's, but it had to wait. It was in square 3/4, nearly halfway down the grid.

The men used hand-held entrenching tools, working slowly to avoid damage. They didn't know if every mound was a grave, how deep the bodies were buried, and whether they were in caskets.

In square 1/1 they removed a rectangular stone with marks that might have once been an inscription but now were indecipherable. The foreman put a colored sticky ID tag on it and laid it to one side. They dug in the hard-packed ground, and at a depth of twenty inches they hit wooden planks so old they crumbled when the spades bit into them. The men swept dirt from the boards and discovered a six-by-two-foot wooden box underneath. They had found their first coffin.

Two men stepped into the hole, removed the rotten planks and swept away more packed soil. Underneath, a twisted body lay on its side, contorted into a fetal position instead of lying straight. Most of the flesh was gone; tufts of hair remained on the grinning skull that looked up at them. The person wore work pants, a cotton shirt and heavy leather boots, all remarkably well preserved after what must have been years underground.

At the medical examiner's direction, the workers donned surgical masks and rubber gloves and carefully removed the body from its grave. They carried it to a nearby area where the ME had set up his workstation. He pinned an ID tag on the corpse's shirt, the same color and number as the one they'd put on the stone.

The work could proceed only as fast as the ME could process the findings, because Landry wanted every disinterred body back in its place before they left at the end of each day. The examinations took time, a lot of notes and photos, and once they had several bodies, they could establish a routine for the exhumations.

Using his phone to record notes, the ME examined the first body while the others searched square 1/1 for more clues. Then they moved to the square marked 1/2, which turned out to be just a grassy space with no stone and, as they found after a little digging, no coffin either.

On their earlier visit, Landry and Em had seen the next two. The stones said JAMES SAVARY MARCH 2009 and K SAVARY JAN 2007.

The crew continued digging. Landry asked Em if she minded seeing a dead body, and she said it was no problem. She'd seen a lot because the cult's custom when someone died was for others to come to a public viewing.

He took her to the doctor's tent, where the first body lay on a table.

"Did you know that man?"

"I'm not sure. He's been dead so long I can't recognize him."

"Is he what you call a Strange One?"

"Yep, but they're usually women. Not so many men. See how twisted up he is? Bet he has a hump on his back."

The ME nodded. "Severely deformed. The way his body was contorted in the coffin, I suspected he might have been buried alive, but now I see what happened. His torso was so convoluted they stuffed him in sideways."

Earlier, Em had said K Savary was a Strange One too, and once they exhumed the body, she turned out to be correct. Although the husband's corpse lay stretched in the coffin to his full six feet, the woman's body was warped and bent like the first one. The Savarys' cadavers and clothing were in much better condition due, the ME said, to their more recent burials.

Around three the ME stopped the exhumations, saying it would take the rest of the day to finish up and rebury the only three bodies they'd found in their first day of effort.

Another deputy arrived at the cemetery as the others were leaving. Junior had sent him to stand guard throughout the night, and Landry appreciated the sheriff's gesture.

There was still plenty of daylight left when everyone boarded the boats and left Asher. The first day was interesting because of the Strange Ones. Nothing else turned up, but they'd finished three graves out of what might end up being a hundred.

The day-shift deputy called Junior, reported on the rather mundane day's activities, and said he'd be back with the others tomorrow.

CHAPTER THIRTY-FOUR

The next morning two people didn't come. Yesterday had been stressful for Em. She and Father Paul stayed in Abbeville, saying they'd come when Landry needed her.

The medical examiner told Landry the first body they'd exhumed was around a hundred years old. The other two had died in 2007 and 2009, and he said the conditions of the bodies bore out those dates.

He took photos and samples of exposed skin, hair and nails. When he finished, two workers laid the bodies back in their coffins, reassembled the wooden slats as best they could, and filled the holes. Others moved ahead with disinterments, and by two in the afternoon, the ME had four more bodies and called a halt to the work. It would take the rest of the afternoon to complete his work.

Since the crew was idle, Landry asked them to work on Billy Whistler's grave. He considered the whole Billy Whistler story a legend created and perpetuated by the cult. The stone read 1883, three years after Asher, and if the grave was empty, there must be a logical reason.

A deformed man had kidnapped Em, but Landry thought it was one of the so-called Strange Ones, sent by Elder Johnson to reclaim the wayward child.

The loose dirt in the grave made digging much easier. Once again they found planks from a top and a four-sided box filled with packed soil. If someone had been buried, there was no body now, just as Em predicted.

They would locate more grid squares devoid of graves, and more graves without stone markers, but this was the only empty grave they would find.

Seventeen days later the crew had finished forty-one of the forty-nine grid squares. They had exhumed fifty-six bodies. Thirty-nine of them, or seventy percent, were so-called Strange Ones. The dates on the stones ranged from 1849 to 2018, and the oldest corpses were so decomposed that the men couldn't remove them. Instead, the ME crawled into the open graves to examine the remains.

As the boats pulled away for the night, a tall man dressed in black stepped out of the trees and walked to the cemetery. He watched them desecrate the graves for several hours, staying far enough into the woods to remain hidden but close enough to hear every comment.

It surprised him that M Savary was helping. After she ran away, he held out hope she was dead. Now that he knew the truth, he considered how to deal with the traitorous girl. He would punish her for her sins, and she would beg for the release of death before it was over.

The man heard an outboard motor, and he walked down the path to Asher to see who had arrived. He stood in the shadows and watched the sheriff pull his boat up to the deputy's, tie it off, and walk through Asher and into the woods.

The sheriff's arrival puzzled him for a moment, but then he understood. Junior wanted to see what progress had been made, how many graves remained closed, and if they'd found anything significant.

They haven't gotten to the important ones yet, the man said to himself.

The sheriff called out to his deputy and said he'd come to make sure Landry was following the court order and not doing things he shouldn't be. He examined the grid system and counted the yet-unopened graves. As he knelt beside the last graves, the tall man nodded. They were the reason the sheriff came, and he could see that they would be opened tomorrow.

The man wondered if Junior would do anything to stop Landry from learning the secrets.

Junior left as the night guard sat in a folding chair and opened his iPad. The deepening shadows overtook the forest and brought the night, and the tall man moved silently through the woods on little-used trails others would have missed. He knew the area so well he could have done it blindfolded. Tomorrow he'd be back to watch the desecrators dig up the last bodies, including the ones that brought the sheriff to Asher.

CHAPTER THIRTY-FIVE

The project was almost over, and Landry felt lost and confused. Three long weeks and a huge amount of Triboro Media's money had perhaps been wasted. He'd worked hunches before, and some didn't pan out, but this had been his most ambitious venture. A handful of grid squares remained to be examined, and he had nothing to show for the effort.

Ted went back to work days ago. Excited at first, he gave up after the grave openings became routine. Except for Strange Ones, the cemetery seemed just like any other, and nothing unusual turned up. Father Paul and Em came every few days, but even she had no role to play when every grave resembled the others.

Film crews from Lafayette, Baton Rouge and Lake Charles came at first, shooting footage and offering enticing ideas about what spooky things the ghost hunter sought. They didn't stay long, and even Landry's station had stopped the nightly updates, because there was nothing happening.

As the crew worked on the few remaining graves, he walked to the shoreline. He needed time to reflect, and perhaps the serenity of the Vermilion River would help sort things in his mind.

In a remarkably short time, he had skyrocketed to fame as a TV personality. Wherever he traveled, people stopped to ask for an autograph or a selfie. His fans called him the ghost hunter, and publicity for the *Bayou Hauntings* series portrayed him as a stellar investigative reporter with a bright future.

He'd fallen for his own hype. He wanted to be all those things, and he confessed to himself that he loved every minute of his newfound stardom. Yes, he'd made amazing discoveries that proved the paranormal to be as real as the things we take for granted, but this time he'd gone way off course. Not every old graveyard yielded paranormal activity. The Sons of Jehovah was a cult with bizarre rituals and practices, but nothing more.

Am I missing something? I thought I'd find answers here — the cult's secrets, a clue about Billy Whistler, and perhaps even more — but this is just a regular cemetery. Decades of intermarriage between close relatives has spawned people the Sons of Jehovah call the Strange Ones, but there's nothing eerie about that. I've wasted enormous effort on a wild-goose chase.

The great Landry Drake had failed. Failure was no stranger earlier in his life, but it seemed bitter and dark now. He smugly talked his boss into this project without doing enough research. Other people made mistakes, not the infallible Landry Drake. But he wasn't infallible, and now he stood in a ghost town that promised to take him down a notch or two.

Part of him wanted to pull the plug now, pack up the equipment, fire the laborers, and walk away. But only a few grids remained. It wouldn't cost much more to go all the way. After this he might write a history of Asher Cemetery. It would be a far cry from the *Bayou Hauntings*, but perhaps that would bring an overambitious man back to reality.

He would finish this project and then he'd take Cate away for a long weekend. She would help him assess things and decide what to do next. Willing himself to concentrate on the project instead of his own thoughts and fears, he returned to the cemetery.

The diggers worked in grid square forty-six, and only three remained. So far this morning they had unearthed three bodies — two of them Strange Ones — and now they moved to the next grave. The medical examiner had time for only one more body today. Regardless of what turned up, everything would end tomorrow.

Filled with melancholy, he watched the crew work and thought about his incredible journey in just twenty-nine years. He might get a job in Galveston to be closer to Cate. That would be one positive thing out of the mess he'd created.

"Landry! Landry, you gotta see this!"

He snapped out of his despondency and ran to Phil, who knelt over a headstone. He did that with every grave marker, getting a good shot before they moved it and unearthed what, if anything, lay beneath.

"Look at this! This is different from anything we've turned up."

You have no idea, thought the man in the forest who watched them.

This stone bore the first complete date they'd come across, and the words set it apart from the rest.

666

Son of the Devil

May 26, 1880

A little light-headed, Landry knelt and ran his fingers over the stone. This grave dated to the night this all began. Supposedly several cult members died, but this one had been no friend. This was a person so despised by the Sons of Jehovah that his grave marker called him the devil's own son.

Em said they'd caught the worst vigilante and hanged him that night. Could this be his grave? Given the inscription, he could think of no other explanation.

Like many of the others, the coffin lid had rotted away. The workers removed the body — most of its exposed flesh had rotted away or been eaten by worms, but there were remnants of a black beard and mustache. After so many years, he still wore a flannel shirt, heavy denim overalls and Western-style boots.

The medical examiner found the clothes interesting. "Of all the cadavers, this is the only one wearing store-bought stuff," he said. "The pants even still have a label." He finished examining the bodies from this morning and turned to this peculiar one.

The work crew moved to the next grid and brushed away a stone inscribed *Justice, 1890*. Here lay another odd stone, next to the Son of the Devil. The excited crew opened the grave and found the body of a man dressed in similar clothes to the last corpse.

All those bodies, and only two wearing store-bought clothes.

This would be the last body for today; the examiner wanted more time on these two. Two grid squares remained, and if nothing unusual happened, they'd wrap things up at Asher tomorrow morning.

The doctor finished and called the group together. Long since accustomed to viewing dead bodies, they gathered close to hear him explain about the "666" body.

"In addition to the store-bought clothes, there are two significant things about the body. First, look at these." He pointed to grooves in the neck. "Ligature marks, consistent with being hanged. I can't say that caused his death, but whatever killed him, he had a rope around his neck at some point.

"Here's the other interesting thing. If he didn't die from hanging, this likely killed him." He pointed to the eyes. "See the damage around the eye sockets? In my opinion someone gouged his eyes out with a stick."

Holy shit, Landry thought. *There's no doubt who this is.* The examiner's next words confirmed it.

"I found this in his pocket," he said, handing Landry an 1846 ten-dollar gold piece with the letters *AWD* carved into the reverse. Both sides of the coin were worn almost smooth.

An exhilarating high replaced the despondency that had engulfed Landry less than an hour ago. Landry pulled out a notebook, thumbed through pages of research notes, and read several entries before he spoke to the group.

He knew who AWD was, and he understood why his gravestone said "666 — Son of the Devil." He'd been the only vigilante captured by the cult that night. Lee said they'd hanged him while his friends rowed away. Em revealed the man they lynched had poked out a girl's eyes. The body itself proved someone gave him a taste of his own medicine.

They had unearthed the corpse of Auguste Dauphin, a blacksmith and one of those who torched Asher on May 26, 1880. From his research, he recalled that Auguste was thirty-four and therefore born in 1846. Over many yearsof rubbing it, the gold good-luck coin he always carried in his pocket had worn smooth.

"He would have been the most hated man in the cult's history," Landry said. "The ones I spoke with who knew Auguste said he did awful things that night. Those things earned him the title 'Son of the Devil' and the number 666 — the Mark of the Beast — on his tombstone. What a way to be remembered."

The tall man hiding in the trees listened as Landry explained his theories to his captivated group of colleagues. He could have walked into the clearing and they wouldn't have noticed. That would happen soon, but not today, because *she* wasn't there.

That grave the best-known one in the cemetery. Every Remembering Day his people gathered around this stone marker and performed a ritual that honored the dead and relived the horrors inflicted on the Sons of Jehovah that night. It was at this grave that the sacrifices were made.

Elder Johnson regretted that there would be no more Remembering Days, but he'd always known it would end someday. One day a person would find a piece, then another, and solve the puzzle. It saddened him that it happened while he was leader — the secret had been kept for fourteen decades — but this was the day, and Landry Drake was the man. If it were possible the elder would stop him, but things had gone too far. They had discovered too much. Perhaps they wouldn't discover the rest, but if they did, so be it. Everything would be revealed and it would truly be over.

Landry and his crew listened to the doctor's report about the second body, the one buried next to Auguste Dauphin. Like the first, this man's eyes had been gouged out. Perhaps that would explain the markings on the gravestone — *Justice, 1890.*

He thought a moment and realized the meaning. Although they didn't know the man, the words made sense. Remembering Day came every ten years. The Asher debacle happened in 1880, so theoretically the first Remembering Day happened in 1890. The man lying on the table before them had been the first victim, a person sacrificed in the name of justice.

The doctor had tallied each body and Landry created a spreadsheet. He examined one hundred fourteen bodies, and all but the last two appeared to be cult members. Fifty-eight of the one hundred twelve were female. Eighty-one of the dead were Strange Ones, mostly females. An astonishing seventy-one percent of the bodies in the cemetery bore the tragic deformities resulting from decades of inbreeding.

Tomorrow would be a short day. They would finish the last two grid squares, pack up their stakes and lines, break down their camp and do a final cleanup. Landry called Father Paul and asked him to bring Em down for the last time.

From his vantage point in the forest, Elder Johnson smiled when he learned the girl would be here. The discoveries they made today saddened him. Perhaps tomorrow would be different — a day of rejoicing for him and his followers.

Landry called Ted and explained about the two important graves. "Send the news crew up here tomorrow, but don't tell them what it's about. If we can keep this quiet, Channel Nine can have this story all to ourselves."

Sheriff Conreco's deputy reported in that evening. "They were excited about two graves," he told his boss. "One was a guy named August or something. The other one didn't have a name, but Landry said neither was a cult member."

Junior couldn't stop things now even if he wanted to. For the last time, he fulfilled his duty to the Conclave. He called Joel Morin.

CHAPTER THIRTY-SIX

The crew felt a sense of accomplishment as they congregated for the last morning at Asher. Everyone moved at an easier pace because the remaining grids wouldn't take long. All the other bodies were back in the earth, their stones placed on freshly turned dirt.

Instead of sending a deputy, the sheriff showed up today. He seemed in a good mood, chatting with some of the laborers and asking Landry if he considered the project successful. Landry admitted after finding the graves of the vigilantes yesterday, things finally began to fall into place. Junior agreed the new graves made things interesting.

His attitude surprised Landry. This was the first civil conversation between them. He seemed different — calm and cordial, as if he wanted to stop the battle. Landry wondered why.

When the final grids produced no bodies, the cleanup process began in earnest. As the men worked, Em and Father Paul walked around the grounds. The elder waited and watched, hoping for an opportunity to snatch her away, but the priest stayed beside her.

It infuriated him to watch her walk to a patch of grass a few yards away. *Damn the girl!* She was going to reveal the last secrets, and he decided to snatch her even with the priest close by. This would be the end of everything, and he must try to stop it.

But Elder Johnson tarried too long. As he prepared to spring from the trees, Em pointed to the ground, said something to Father Paul, and he yelled for Landry to come.

He cursed himself for his indecision. It seemed they might miss the other graves, but the wretched child had ruined that possibility. Elder Johnson calmed himself. That impetuous move would have been suicidal with so many people around. He would capture her soon, and she would pay the price for this sin and her others.

"There's more graves there," she announced, pointing out a group of stones in the tallgrass. "I forgot about them. I'm not sure why they're away from the others, but they were part of Remembering Day too."

Landry assembled the crew; they thought they were finished, but here were more graves. He only had a few days left on his exhumation permit, but it appeared this small plot wouldn't take much time.

Before the diggers began, Landry examined each grave, taking notes and pictures. He found eleven stones unlike the ones in the cemetery proper. Identical in size and shape, each bore a single inscription — a year. The first read 1890, and there was one almost every ten years afterwards from 1900 to 2010. Three years in the sequence were missing, and by the time he'd finished, he understood why this place existed. No grave markers existed for 1930, 1950 and 2000 because those dead girls had been dumped on the shore to be found. The eleven graves in the tallgrass belonged to eleven girls who vanished without a trace.

His men must stand down; there would be no digging here. Landry couldn't allow it because the court ordered exhumations didn't apply. These weren't deceased cult members. These graves contained eleven girls who were kidnapped, mutilated and murdered by a creature called Billy Whistler. This was the last piece of the puzzle. He conferred with the sheriff, who radioed for help.

Remembering Day happened every ten years on May 26, a memorial to the burning of Asher. With three exceptions, a body lay in this plot from each Remembering Day since 1890.

Elder Johnson moved silently through the trees, getting closer to the group to hear them. Landry asked Em about Remembering Day 2010, the only one she attended.

"Do you remember a frightened girl, maybe a prisoner?"

She didn't question how he knew that. "Yeah, the girl who died wasn't one of us."

The girl who died? "What happened to her?"

"Elder Johnson gave her to Billy Whistler, same as every other Remembering Day."

"And what did he do?"

Em stood in silence a moment and then she walked a few feet. She pointed to the ground.

"He dug her eyes out and then they buried her right there."

CHAPTER THIRTY-SEVEN

Junior's life spun madly like a whirlpool toward a deep, dark hole at the bottom. Three personas lived in his body, each pulling him in a different direction.

First, he was a human being with a conscience, a clear understanding of right and wrong, and a genuine desire not to create pain and suffering for other people. He wanted to do the right thing, but his other roles pulled him away from decency and civility.

He also served as a member of the Conclave and Joel Morin's errand boy. It embarrassed him to be involved with a group that should never have begun, much less been perpetuated all these years. So what if his great-grandfather did some despicable things a long, long time ago — what did it matter? He wondered if people would hold him personally responsible for things that happened a hundred and something years ago. Surely the voters wouldn't run him out of office if the truth came out.

He told himself that often, although sometimes when he couldn't sleep, he realized he must answer for the sins of the fathers, because they were his sins too — his and the other Conclave members.

Lastly, long ago Junior put his hand on a Bible and swore to uphold the laws he then violated over and over. People in Abbeville considered him a decent man. How surprised and disappointed they would be to learn the truth.

The truth would be revealed soon because of what the cult girl showed Landry today. People had died on Junior's watch, and those deaths could have been prevented if a Conclave member with decency and courage stopped this long ago. But no member exhibited those qualities, and the horrors continued.

Even though he was chairman, Joel and David Hebert had lesser roles — they merely kept the secrets. Junior's involvement was much greater. The family of a missing girl had come to him in tears, trusting him as sheriff to do the right thing. But he maneuvered the facts, steered them in the wrong direction, and kept the secrets intact. They would never find their daughter, but he had done right by the Conclave.

Governor Ferrara had reason to worry about the truth coming out, because his great-uncle had been the sheriff in 1880. The man responsible for law and order in Vermilion Parish was an accessory to seven murders, and he did nothing to stop Auguste Dauphin from raping and blinding a girl. The cowardly perpetrators swore an oath of silence because their lives would have been over otherwise.

That sheriff, the governor's ancestor, kept the secret when Auguste's wife reported him missing. The man witnessed the hanging but said nothing. To compound the crime, he eliminated the wife too.

Each of those men had been responsible for the atrocities that awful night, just as the Conclave was responsible today. None of them had the guts to step forward and confess what had happened and who had been there.

The day Landry Drake came to Vermilion Parish was the day everything started to change. Junior had been furious when Landry showed up in Abbeville, but in a rare period of self-examination, he admitted he was afraid of being found out. He'd carried the burden for twenty-seven years, since the day his father lay on his deathbed and passed the awful mantle of secrecy to his unwitting son.

Junior lay in bed, again unable to sleep because of living nightmares he carried inside. But this night was different. He had an overpowering premonition that something was about to happen. Things were coming to a head, and there was nothing he could — or would — do to stop them. Landry Drake had come for a reason, but he also had done something else. He had opened the floodgates that would put an end to all this.

Junior decided he would write everything down tomorrow — what he knew about the Conclave and its members then and now, the truth about that night in Asher, and why he was ready to come clean. That document might well become his life insurance policy.

The phone rang next to his bed. The hour was late, and a powerful feeling swept through his body. If he answered, it would be an irreversible decision. The person he had been yesterday would be no more.

Junior felt a calmness sweep over him; it was time. He answered and a familiar voice said, "Sheriff? This is Landry. I need your help."

CHAPTER THIRTY-EIGHT

On his way back from Asher, Landry got a call from Darlene at Caldwell House. Someone had dropped a letter addressed to him through the front mail slot. By now people knew where Landry stayed when he came to town, so it didn't surprise him. He stopped by and picked it up.

Handwritten words in flourishing calligraphy filled a note card.

There is much you do not know, and you are in danger. To learn everything, come to Asher tomorrow at midnight. Come by boat, and alone. Watch for my signal. Tell no one.

Interesting. Who wrote it, and what did it mean? Could he find more answers, or was he walking into a trap?

The story wasn't finished, and so he would go, but not alone. The person he wanted along had been his fiercest enemy since the day Landry first came to Vermilion Parish. Should he involve the sheriff? Until today, he wouldn't have considered it, but the change in Junior's attitude at the cemetery this afternoon convinced him to do it. He made the call.

At 11:30 he started the engine of a rented bass boat and pulled away from the Perry dock. A long rope led to a canoe in tow. Junior sat in it, holding an oar in his lap.

In the stillness, anyone on shore would hear his approach. He kept the motor steady as he released the canoe a quarter mile from Asher. At the last turn, he looked back and saw Junior quietly paddling downstream.

At Asher a light in the woods flashed once, twice, three times. He cut power, let the boat drift to shore, and tied it up. As he crawled through the fence, three flashes came from the trail that led to the cemetery.

Landry wondered about the deputy Junior had posted at the graveyard. It appeared he was being lured to the graveyard, but wouldn't the guard be watching?

Three more flashes came from somewhere down the trail.

Junior would be five minutes behind him, heading toward the cemetery if he didn't see Landry at Asher. Armed with that knowledge, Landry kept moving. He illuminated his light and followed the path. Pale moonbeams illuminated the graveyard where his crew had worked.

No one was there, including the deputy. He turned the light off.

"Deputy? It's Landry Drake. Where are you?"

A voice came from the opposite side of the cemetery. "Thank you for coming, Mr. Drake. The deputy has been detained, I'm afraid. I appreciate your bringing someone with you. You performed well, just as I expected." In the gloom he noticed the silhouette of a man wearing a tall hat.

"I didn't bring anyone —"

"Please don't insult me. Do you not think I would be ready for you? Now your friend approaches; it is time."

Something connected with the side of Landry's head, sending waves of flashing lights cascading through his brain. He fell to the ground unconscious, so he didn't feel his body being dragged into the woods.

Only five minutes behind Landry, Junior pulled the canoe onshore into some bushes, knelt and listened for voices. Then he walked through the ruins and down the path into the clearing where the graves lay. He pulled out his service revolver and whispered Landry's name.

Nothing.

This time he shouted, but the only sounds were the rustling and trilling of night creatures. In just five minutes, Landry had vanished.

A voice behind him said, "Mr. Drake can't help you now."

Junior raised his weapon and wheeled around, but he saw nothing.

"Landry! Landry, where are you?" Someone groaned nearby. As he took a step toward the sound, he noticed something. He turned just as a man swung an axe handle. As the wooden handle connected with his right arm, he pulled the trigger. The gunshot reverberated through the trees, scattering birds everywhere. He screamed in pain, dropped the gun, and fell to the ground, writhing in agony.

Two men stood over him. The one who had spoken earlier said, "Tie his hands. We must go."

Landry woke with a monster headache. He lay on damp leaves in the forest. His eyes refused to focus; he touched the side of his head, and his hand came away bloody.

Was there a gunshot? Perhaps. Fuzzy memories reformed slowly. The sheriff. The cemetery. A man speaking to him, then pain and blackness.

Where was Junior? Had he been shot?

He pushed himself to a sitting position, groaned with pain, and tried to shake the dizziness from his head. He glanced down and noticed a piece of paper sticking out of his shirt pocket. With the light on his phone, he read words penned by the same hand as before.

Your associate will be released unharmed if you meet these demands.

First, you will reveal nothing about what you found at Asher and leave the parish.

Second, your investigation will stop at once, and you will give your word to disclose nothing about the Sons of Jehovah, the legends you incorrectly think you understand, information you have learned, or anything else about this matter. There will be no television show, ever. It is over, Mr. Drake, at least for you.

Once you have left the parish for good, I will release the person who accompanied you. If you break your word, grave harm will befall people you hold dear.

He stood and discovered he was only a few yards from the graveyard. They had dragged him into the woods and taken Junior away. He staggered into the clearing and saw the gun lying in the grass. His head throbbed again as he bent to pick it up, and he heard a noise.

He waited and heard it again — a groan and a weak "help."

The deputy lay on the ground across the clearing. Someone had ambushed him and knocked him out.

Once again because of Landry, someone else was in danger — or worse — and he must do something about it. Hopefully Junior's resourcefulness would keep him alive. The man might be overweight and out of shape, but he had been trained in law enforcement.

He suggested the deputy phone his dispatcher; lots of people monitored the radio channels, and this explosive information needed to stay under wraps for as long as possible.

Junior's kidnapping threw his department into high gear. The chief deputy — Junior's second-in-command — assembled every man on the force. Riot gear in hand, they boarded boats to go to Asher.

The sheriff's department would help rescue Junior, and now Landry had an obligation to fulfill. He called Channel Nine's news director and explained the evening's events. With a story like this, the first ones on the scene got the scoop, and he provided the contact information for the man with the airboat who could bring them to Asher quickly. He called Father Paul, who said he'd hitch a ride on the airboat too.

They heard the sound of motors, and in a moment two massive searchlights panned the shoreline. The deputy waved them in, and six of Junior's men stepped onshore from two VPSO boats. Landry gave the lead deputy a summary of where things stood.

"We need to get moving fast," the leader said. "Time's critical. They can't have gotten far on foot, but the more lead time they have, the worse it may be for Sheriff Conreco."

The young deputy assumed command well, Landry observed. This was the first real assignment he'd ever had on a small-town force run by a domineering sheriff, and his first job was to find his own boss. Landry offered to help him, and the deputy gratefully accepted.

The airboat pulled to shore, offloading Landry's cameraman Phil Vandegriff, a news crew, and Father Paul. It surprised Landry to see Em with him, and he asked why the priest brought her.

"If they took him to New Asher, she thinks she can lead us there. She agreed, but she's terrified they may capture her. I promised we'd keep her safe, and she doesn't have to go all the way. Once we get close, I'll bring her back.

"The night Em ran away, she walked for miles along a highway. I say we let her lead us and see if anything jogs her memory."

The muffled tone of a cell phone came from somewhere in the grass. A deputy saw it and recognized it belonged to Junior. He handed it to the leader, who passed it to Landry.

The missed call was from someone named Joel Morin. He put the phone in his pocket, but it rang again right away.

"Landry Drake."

There was a pause, and then a refined older man's voice said, "Let me talk to Junior Conreco."

"Who's this?"

"Put him on the phone." The man's tone was curt and demanding, and it struck Landry the wrong way. "I don't have time for this," he replied, cutting off the call and pocketing the phone.

Joel was angry. What was Landry Drake doing with the sheriff's phone? Lately Junior had seemed introspective, and he'd even questioned Joel's orders. Had he told the reporter their secrets? Had he unlocked doors that were best left closed?

The news crew and two deputies stayed behind, because Landry thought rescuing Junior might require stealth instead of an army.

Em searched the trees at the back of the cemetery and located a half-hidden trail, one she said the people used when they came to Asher for Remembering Day. This was the way to go, and they started on their journey. Em and Father Paul led the way, followed by Landry and Phil, who would shoot video as they walked. The lead deputy and four others brought up the rear.

CHAPTER THIRTY-NINE

Junior awoke, recalling someone had spoken to him in the graveyard.

Flashing bolts of pain shot through his pounding head as he was jostled. He lay tied on a makeshift stretcher that two men were carrying. Noticing he had awakened, they dropped it roughly to the ground.

He cried out in pain and croaked, "Where … where am I?"

A tall man wearing a hat said, "Stand him up. If he can walk, we can make better time."

Two men jerked him upright. He stumbled, but they squeezed his arms to keep him erect.

"Walk."

Men in black surrounded him, and when the two holding him released their grips, he teetered.

"I said walk!"

He took a step, then another, and then his knees gave way.

"Deacon Abner, Deacon Gabriel, get on either side of him and walk him along. He'll regain his footing soon. We haven't far to go."

The trees ended at a paved two-lane road, and the men walked to a spot in the trees where three horses nibbled the grass. They put the sheriff on a horse, tied his hands behind his bank, and a man climbed into the saddle in front of him. The other two mounted their horses, and they rode off into the night.

He felt better but with his hands tethered, he could do nothing. As they rode along the highway, he thought he might catch a driver's attention, but traffic was sparse on this country road an hour before daybreak. Occasionally a pickup passed, country music blaring and horn honking as it flew past on the deserted highway.

They left the road, guided the horses through a swampy field, and followed a path into another forest. The sun rose as they rode on and came to a man standing on the pathway.

"All clear?"

"Quiet, Elder Johnson. Been quiet since you left."

Elder Johnson. Junior was in grave danger. They hadn't killed him outright, which meant they had something else in mind, and he must stay alert. He didn't know Landry's situation or if anyone was aware he had been kidnapped, but none of that mattered. To survive, he must escape.

They rode into a town cut from the forest. Wooden buildings stood on three sides of a grassy square. There were shops and residences, and Junior knew he was in New Asher. He wondered if their old town looked like this before the vigilantes destroyed it.

In the middle of the square stood an elevated platform with a staircase and a floored second story. He thought it might be a place where people gave speeches, but he realized it looked more like a gallows from a movie set.

As men hauled him up the stairs and tethered him to a corner pole, he struggled to remain calm. He whispered encouraging words he hoped were true. He wasn't in the remote boondocks of *Deliverance*. This was Vermilion Parish, Louisiana, in the twenty-first century.

I'll be okay. I'm probably still in the parish, near some town. Someone will find me. I'll bet they're already looking.

Despite his attempt at optimism, frightening possibilities preyed at his mind. He forced his thoughts onto rescue and friends and home. And how he would stay alive if Elder Johnson Lafont learned who he was.

Unfortunately for the sheriff, the elder realized whom he'd captured the moment he laid eyes on Junior. Of all people Landry could have brought along, this man was perfect. The elder had captured one of the Conclave members at last.

CHAPTER FORTY

Landry and the others walked through dense forest for two miles and emerged onto highway 330, which Em claimed was the road she'd walked along that night. She led them south as she looked for another trail that would lead into another woods.

A man in a northbound pickup noticed the deputies' uniforms. He stopped, rolled down the window, and said, "Y'all looking for somethin'?"

"We're looking for some people who may have committed a crime. Have you seen anything unusual?"

"I just might have. I noticed four men on horseback going south on the highway about an hour ago. I passed them, but I didn't stop because I had a deadline to drop some produce in Henry. They looked like they were in a movie, all dressed in black. The guy in front had one of them old-fashioned tall hats. And there was a guy riding behind one of the others."

The man hadn't gotten a good look at the fourth rider, but Landry thought it might be Junior. As the driver pulled away, he urged everyone to move along as fast as possible. Time might be running out.

Junior's phone rang again; it was the same caller, and Landry wanted to know who he was.

"Good luck finding the sheriff, Mr. Drake."

"How in hell —"

He could sense satisfaction in the man's reply. "You're all over the news, Mr. Drake. When you find him — *if* you find him — tell him to contact me immediately."

"Who are you?" he shouted, but the man had hung up.

Father Paul called out, "Come over here! Over here, everyone!" Em had found a trail. Landry knew it was the right one — he saw fresh hoofmarks in the soft dirt.

"It's not far now," the girl said. "You go straight down this trail until you get to the town. I don't want to go on from here."

The lead deputy called for a cruiser, and Em and Father Paul walked to a shady spot to wait.

Landry checked the GPS; they were only ten miles from Erath and Delcambre. It was time for reinforcements. Junior was in New Asher, and he had to be ready for anything.

The lead deputy notified the state police, the sheriff in neighboring Iberia Parish, and the Erath and Delcambre cops. He gave them GPS coordinates for an assembly point and asked that they hustle when he gave the signal.

Ten minutes later Landry heard something and shushed the others.

There were voices coming from far away — too great a distance to understand the words.

They tiptoed along the trail and froze in place when they saw buildings in a clearing. Junior stood on the second floor of a wooden structure, tied to a post but looking okay. Men with pitchforks milled about in the square below, waiting for something.

"Should we go in?" the deputy whispered, but Landry shook his head.

"Not yet. We don't have enough men. I can see thirty, maybe forty of the cult guys, and there's bound to be more around the town. Send our location to the others, and we'll wait until they get here."

A few minutes later when things turned really nasty, he wished to God he'd called in reinforcements earlier.

CHAPTER FORTY-ONE

Just then the square filled with frenzied activity. The pathetic misfits Em called Strange Ones, mostly women and children but also a few men, were easy to recognize. They stood by themselves, shunned by the so-called normal ones. These pathetic people had stooped backs, and their arms dragged on the ground. Most were ragged and dirty, indicating that others in their clan refused to give them even basic care.

Elder Johnson climbed the wooden ladder and stood beside the sheriff. He spoke to his followers in a commanding voice. "This is a day of celebration like no other! Behold this man, whose ancestor killed our people and sacked our town. Revenge will soon be ours!"

He worked the crowd, using the intonations of his voice to incite his people.

In a moment a loud, warbling whistle echoed through the town square and into the woods where Landry's group waited. Elder Johnson's people fell quiet and waited. The deputies looked at Landry, but there was no time to explain.

"This day shall go down as our finest," the elder screamed, raising both hands into the air like a modern-day Moses. "Behold what a fine new prize we have!"

He climbed down the ladder and the men gathered around him in anticipation. Not allowed to join in the festivities, the women stood to one side and watched.

A bizarre hunchbacked thing emerged from the forest opposite where Landry stood. It resembled the Strange Ones, but more grotesque and filthy. As twisted and wiry as the creature was, it was also strong. It toted Em's unconscious body on his back in a fireman's carry, loping along easily despite the added weight.

Landry panicked. Em was in imminent peril, but what had Billy Whistler done with Father Paul? He pulled the pistol from his belt. They must do something, but there were seven against dozens of pitchfork-wielding cultists. He waited for an opportunity.

The mob shouted praises for the child's return, and Elder Johnson went to the creature, touched its arm and said something. It seemed to understand, made a guttural noise and dropped Em to the ground. Landry could see deep gouges on its face and arm. He knew they were from 1921 when a hunter claimed to have slashed a rougarou with his knife.

Em opened her eyes and looked up at Elder Johnson. An unearthly, pitiful wail came from her lips. It surprised Landry that she feared the elder more than the hideous Billy Whistler, who loped off into the woods, whistling his now-familiar call.

There was a rustling sound behind Landry. Someone was moving down the trail toward them. A deputy pulled his gun, and for a split-second Landry thought everything was over. The lawman held his fire as Father Paul came around a bend, his chest heaving. "They knocked me out and left me in the trees next to the highway," he whispered.

"When I awoke, I couldn't find Em. I followed the trail. Thank God you're here. Is she with you?"

Landry pointed, and the priest gasped as they watched Elder Johnson drag Em to the middle of the square. "Bring the cage and back off so all can see!"

They shouted and chanted as the helpless sheriff watched from the structure above. Landry understood how he felt, because his men could do nothing either.

Em shouted, "Not the cage! Please don't do that to me!" She struggled and tried to pull away from his viselike grip, but she was no match for him. Two men brought a wire kennel — a crate intended for a large dog — and he forced her into it. She was bent like a pretzel, crouched with her bowed head touching her knees, and with her bottom resting on her heels. Her hands were at her sides, and there wasn't an extra inch of room anywhere.

"Please, please," she mumbled, her voice muffled now.

Landry seethed as he watched the elder, and he wondered how many times she and others had endured this inhumane confinement.

Elder Johnson pointed to one of his men and bellowed, "You're in charge of her punishment. Guard her. If she escapes again, *you* get the cage!" He turned to the women and commanded, "Mock her!"

It was obvious this was a familiar ritual. All the women — Strange Ones and the others — gathered around the cage and taunted her, calling her a whore and a traitor. "Barren," they hissed. Landry understood how much the words hurt Em, because she had said barrenness was a sin. They spat on her and kicked the sides of the cage while the child, unable to move, had to take whatever abuse they dished out.

Landry's men waited in the woods just fifty feet away, but it might as well have been a thousand. From his perch Junior shouted, "What are you doing, you bastard? Stop hurting her!"

Her guard taunted the sheriff. "Elder knows what's best for errant children. She'll learn her lesson, that one. And then you'll learn yours!"

Elder Johnson opened the cage and prodded Em out with a stick, like he was curbing a mongrel. "Is everyone ready to give our little traitor her punishment?" he yelled.

More and more frenzied, the crowd screamed like madmen and women. They moved toward Em, who lay huddled on the ground, quivering with fear.

He kicked her with his boot, turned to a nearby man, and said, "Deacon Joshua, I choose your son to perform the ritual."

A strapping youth in his twenties, barefooted and wearing overalls, stepped forward. He looked worried, hesitant.

The elder said, "Be proud, my son. This is an honor. Do you wish to use the knife, or will you use the pitchfork?"

The boy didn't seem proud at all; he looked terrified, but he knew the ritual. He must have seen it before. "The knife, Elder. I will use the knife."

A deacon handed the young man a sheath. He pulled out a long Bowie knife, its twelve-inch blade gleaming in the half-light. He walked toward Em, and those surrounding her moved back further, giving him room and allowing the expectant crowd to see. Excited murmurs echoed throughout the square.

This was like Jonestown — the people drank the Kool-Aid and they would do whatever Elder Johnson commanded.

Landry couldn't wait any longer. The elder was too far away for a clear shot, so he fired twice into the air.

The people shouted in alarm and ran about. They looked up to be sure their prisoner remained secure. The men pulled out their own knives, as did Elder Johnson, who commanded the women with straight backs to surround him. It occurred to Landry that this was something they'd practiced. Use the women as a human shield to protect the elder. Johnson Lafont was no commander — he was nothing but a coward.

"Kill the girl!" the elder shouted, but in the confusion the young man had dropped the knife. He bent, picked it up, and stood as another shot rang out, this one hitting its mark. The boy's head exploded, and the people screamed in terror. Elder Johnson shouted for them to remain calm, but it had no effect on the confused, frightened mob.

Landry had gotten off a shot, and he shouted, "Give it up! You don't have a chance!" He motioned to the others, who shouted too.

They remained hidden, and the elder didn't know how many of them were out there. He raised his knife defiantly and screamed, "If you make a move, everyone will die! Men, take your women and defend our honor!"

As if performing a drill they'd practiced many times, the men ran here and there, finding their wives, grabbing them from behind, and holding knives at their necks. It was a surreal sight that sickened Landry. Em had described women as nothing but chattel, and he was seeing it play out in real life.

Landry fired another shot, and one woman surrounding Elder Johnson fainted. Thinking she had been hit, he struggled to pull another one into the void she had created. The deacons looked at the elder and each other in alarm, while taking their attention off Em and Phil. Landry seized the opportunity in the confusion.

"Run!" he yelled, and his men rushed into the square.

Landry had run track in high school, but he never sprinted faster than today. He flew through the air, body-slamming Elder Johnson to the ground, and the women surrounding him backed away. He grabbed the elder's knife and ordered him to stand.

As Landry moved, Father Paul overpowered the distracted man closest to Em and knelt to cradle her trembling body in his arms. The deputies stood together scanning the crowd, pistols ready, while Phil climbed the ladder and untied the sheriff. They rushed down and joined the others.

A few deacons tried to overpower the deputies; they paused when Landry shouted, "Stop! It's over!"

They turned toward their leader and saw Landry behind him, holding a knife to his throat. He yelled, "Drop your weapons, now!" But it didn't work. Unsure, the deacons looked to the elder and waited.

Even with his own life in danger, Elder Johnson was hell-bent on vengeance against the child defector. "Kill the girl!" he shouted in defiance.

Before anyone could react, a deacon pushed Father Paul aside, fell on Em, and plunged his knife into the girl's midsection. She gasped in astonishment, looked at the blood forming on her dress, and fell back, still. Screaming a feral cry that came from somewhere deep in his heart, the priest jerked the man away, took the knife, and drove it deep into his heart. He tossed the body aside like garbage and tore open Em's dress to locate her wound. He felt her shallow breaths as he held her close and pleaded with her to hang on.

Moving about wildly, the people shouted and wailed. Landry screamed, "It's over!" as he kept the knife tight against Elder Johnson's throat. "Your leader is an evil man, and he is accountable. None of you are to blame. You did what you were told. Drop your weapons now and you'll be free!"

These people were unaccustomed to independent thinking. Some followed his order and put down their knives and pitchforks, but most waited for orders from Johnson Lafont.

The elder's hands were at his sides. He slipped one into a pocket, and before Landry realized what was happening, he raised his hand to his mouth, slipped something inside, and shouted, "It is truly over!" He crunched his teeth and Landry felt the man's body go rigid in seconds. The tyrannical leader of the Sons of Jehovah fell to the ground, a gutless coward even in death.

His followers stared in shock at their fallen leader, and one by one, they dropped their weapons. There was silence at first, but then the women began to weep. Landry assumed they were grieving as their murmurs intensified into shrieks. The females became fully human for the first time.

The only thing women knew of the outside world was what their husbands reported after trips to buy supplies. They would whisper among themselves, wondering what it would be like to be whole — to be equal to their husbands. But they dared not let Elder Johnson hear, because they would be beaten for such thinking.

Now the women rejoiced, shouting and hugging each other while their husbands looked on in astonishment. The men's will to fight had died along with the leader who subjugated them their entire lives.

The women were a different thing. Forcing women into submission was biblical, or so Elder Johnson preached. They watched their wives assert themselves, and the behavior baffled them.

"Hallelujah," an older woman said in a hesitant voice, testing her newfound freedom.

Another voice, even louder. "Praise Jehovah!"

A younger one shouted, "Can it be true? Is it over?"

Someone screamed, "It *is* over! Hallelujah indeed!"

As the women experienced an awakening, one man gathered others around him. He pointed at the sheriff and spoke words Landry couldn't hear. It appeared he was spurring them to action, because some picked up the weapons they had dropped.

Confused, Landry yelled, "What are you doing? You're free. It's over!"

"Not for him," another deacon shouted. "Elder told us his ancestor was one of the evil ones, and he must pay. Kill him!"

"Their blood runs in his veins!"

"Yes, kill him!"

"He must die!"

The mob scene Landry had just put down rose again with a cacophony of screams and cries. Men with knives moved toward Junior. He had no weapon, and he walked to Landry's side.

Landry had to get things back under control. "All that happened before this man was born. He's not to blame!"

His words didn't work. Landry took the sheriff by the arm, held the gun high in the air, and shouted, "Look at me!"

Thank goodness the men still followed directions without thinking. They paused and looked his way. Landry lowered the pistol and put it on the ground in front of the sheriff and himself.

"You must stop this right now. You're free men and women — Elder Johnson doesn't control you. This man doesn't deserve to die. Yes, someone in his family did an awful thing at Asher, but his only sin was keeping it a secret. He never knew that relative, just like you never knew your neighbors whom they murdered that night. It happened a hundred and forty years ago. He isn't responsible for the sins of his fathers, and God won't allow you to punish him for them.

"Tonight this man atoned for what his ancestors did. He and I came to save each of you from imprisonment and torture, but your elder captured him. That man treated you like slaves. Women, he never even gave you a name. He forced young girls to bear children to perpetuate the cult. That's wrong; men and women don't have to be slaves. You don't deserve to live like that, and thanks to Sheriff Conreco and these others, you're free. He blames himself for keeping the secret, but now all of us will help you live the rest of your lives without fear."

With no time to prepare, he had chosen his words well. The murmuring continued, but he could feel the tension dissipate. Men put down their weapons, women hugged their children close, and the crowd dispersed, although no one would go near Junior, who was still the devil to them.

In the midst of the confusion, Landry had forgotten about his other adversary. He heard the warble seconds before Billy Whistler tore from the shadows. He raced like a wolf across the square and jumped full-bore into Junior Conreco's chest. In seconds the creature's long fingernails tore Junior's shirt apart and dug deep gashes into his skin. Junior fell backwards and Billy Whistler landed on top of him, furiously scratching and clawing.

"Shoot him!" Conreco screamed, and Landry dived for the gun he'd placed on the ground. A former deputy, he was familiar with guns, but he must be close to not hit the sheriff. He drew near and raised the weapon, but Billy Whistler looked his way and sprang through the air like a banshee.

The creature's claws extended, and its mouth twisted into a deadly grimace as it flew towards Landry. He fired shot after shot into the body hurtling toward him until he heard clicks. Em had said it was impossible to kill the thing. He hoped she was wrong.

Momentum propelled the disgusting creature toward Landry, and as the thing struck him, they fell backwards. He could smell its fetid breath on his face as it raised its claws to strike. The bullets hadn't worked.

A face flashed through his mind — a face he knew.

Use the potion.

He grabbed the glass ampule, aimed it at Billy Whistler's face, and pressed the plunger hard. A spray of beautiful purple flowers shot from the vial deep into the beast's throat. It gave a fierce snarl, and Landry tensed for the fatal blow, but he felt the sinewy limbs sag. He gave a mighty push and shoved the nasty being to the ground beside him. Gasping, he lay back and felt his chest. His shirt was in shreds, but the claws had missed his body.

I'll be damned. The stuff actually worked.

He went to see about Junior, who was trying to sit up. His shirt was in shreds, and blood ran from several gashes in his chest and arms. "I'll be all right," the sheriff moaned. "Take care of the girl."

CHAPTER FORTY-TWO

Too late to quell the mob, the scene became chaotic once again as reinforcements rushed in from every direction.

Three of Junior's deputies ran out of the woods wearing helmets and flak jackets and with weapons drawn. Delcambre and Erath policemen joined the Iberia Parish sheriff and his deputies. The worst of it had ended, and the help they needed came from two EMTs they brought. After a quick assessment, one knelt to treat Em and the other went to Junior's side.

Em lay in Father Paul's arms while the medic cleaned her wound. Her condition was serious, but the knife appeared to have missed her vital organs. He radioed for a medical chopper. The sheriff's injuries were painful but less severe; the other EMT cleaned and bandaged the gouges in his chest and arms and said his next stop would be Abbeville General for antibiotics and a tetanus shot.

Landry examined the place where he'd tossed Billy Whistler's body, but the creature had disappeared. The terrifying thought that Billy remained alive went through his mind as he ran to the place and found a large pile of dust. The one-hundred-thirty-six-year-old monster's body had disintegrated the moment he ingested the wolfsbane.

Lost in thought, Father Paul held Em's hand. He had killed a human being — an act both justified and necessary — but he had broken one of the Ten Commandments. He was a man of the cloth who had dedicated his life to the Lord's work, but he was a sinner of the worst kind — a murderer.

Phil asked Landry how he killed Billy Whistler. "I thought you were a goner. The bullets didn't stop him, but then something happened — I couldn't see what — and he fell dead."

"The more I heard about the Strange Ones and their short lifespans, the more I knew Billy was something different. There's a resemblance, but if Em's correct — and I think now she is — he's been around since before the fire at Asher. I became convinced he was the thing behind the rougarou legend — and perhaps he was a werewolf.

"I visited an old voodoo priest, explained my situation, and he said only one thing will stop werewolves. Wolfsbane — pretty purple flowers that are fatal to them. He sold me the wolfsbane and an ampule to launch them with. It sounded like mumbo jumbo, but it was my only shot. And by God, it worked. Crazy."

"Crazy is right," Phil commented as a cult member approached them.

Unused to seeing strangers, most of the townspeople stood at a distance, waiting and watching. An older man walked across the square with a swagger reminiscent of Elder Johnson's. He marched to Landry and put his face into the reporter's.

"I'm Deacon Abner Savary. Actually, elder now, since Johnson's dead and I'm next in line." He pointed to Em and said, "That girl belongs to us. She stays here; you ain't takin' her away."

A moan escaped Em's lips as the medic secured her to a stretcher.

The priest snapped, "She's eighteen years old and she can make her own decisions. She's been through enough hell with you people. She's coming with us, and no one will stand in her way."

The deacon stood his ground for a moment, pondering what he should do, but he stood down and walked away. Landry breathed a sigh of relief, hoping now it truly was all over, as Elder Johnson proclaimed when he swallowed the poison pill.

As the new elder ordered his people back to their homes, the lawmen prepared to return to civilization. Junior's lead deputy got word by radio that a state police chopper was inbound — late because they came from further away. They were too late to quell the riot, but the helicopter would carry the others out.

The medivac chopper landed in the clearing, sending the cult members fleeing to their homes in a panic. They loaded Em on a stretcher, but Junior refused to go, saying he would stay at New Asher until the rescuers and lawmen left. The EMT checked his bandages again and said he'd be fine to wait a few hours before going to the emergency room.

The sun was up, its rays making the atmosphere heavy and steamy. Landry's body ached for caffeine, but coffee wasn't on the menu in New Asher. As they waited for the state police helicopter, Junior told Landry he had something to say.

"I made you into my adversary. I did everything in my power to throw you off track, but tonight you saved my life. I've realized something. It's time for me to get everything off my chest at last. I'll do it the minute I get back to Abbeville, before I go home. These secrets have weighed me down for too many years.

"I want you to be there when I tell my story. Father Paul too — there's a lot of confessing that's got to happen before I can ever hold my head up again. You're going to do a show about Asher — how can you not? But you only have half the story. I'm ready to tell you the rest."

Junior had found peace. He'd carried a burden for people dead for generations, and it was time to let things go. To keep the Conclave's secrets, he had harassed and intimidated people who didn't deserve it — people like Catfish Guidry and countless others over the years. He had been under Joel Morin's thumb for ages, he had tolerated the snooty, simple-minded undertaker David Hebert, and he had given deference to the governor, a man no better than he was.

A weight was lifted from his shoulders. He would tell the truth, and secret pacts be damned. God only knew what a struggle it was to keep everything locked deep inside.

CHAPTER FORTY-THREE

Three men — Landry, Father Paul and Junior — sat in the sheriff's office with the door closed. A pot of coffee would keep them alert, and a recorder on the desk would capture what the sheriff had to say.

My story begins on May 26, 1880. Just after midnight, five drunken men took the law into their own hands. One despicable act followed another that fateful night, each worse than the last until one of them made a fateful decision that would impact many lives from that day until this. I will explain how I learned this story when I've finished telling it.

Simon Navarro was my great-grandfather, and he lived his entire miserable life with nothing to show for it except for one horrific accomplishment. Nobody found out what he and four others did that night in a town downriver from Abbeville called Asher. That was the biggest thing he did in his entire life, and it was a terrible accomplishment.

The vigilantes — for that is what they were —told their wives they'd be home by two, figuring it would take twenty minutes to get to Asher, twenty minutes to torch the town's buildings, and twenty minutes to return, with an extra hour built in for contingencies. Now it was after four, the men were very late, and five women worried over their missing husbands.

The men had planned to be back long before sunrise, because by then there would be activity on the dock in Abbeville. They couldn't risk being identified by some do-gooder who'd label them criminals instead of what they considered themselves to be — soldiers for the Lord. But things hadn't gone as they had hoped.

Everything went well at first. Although seriously intoxicated, each man somehow made it to shore upright and undetected. As they expected, the town was quiet. It surprised them how many buildings they saw; they counted more than a dozen commercial structures fronting a broad dirt street, and as they walked, they tossed gasoline here and there. They fanned out, dousing every third or fourth house. It was a windy night and the flames would spread in an instant. They didn't intend to kill anyone; they would ignite the gasoline, run to the boats, and shout an alarm as they pulled away. People would have time to flee before the flames spread to the houses, and in the confusion the perpetrators would escape into the night.

At that moment their luck ran out. Just as they prepared to light the fires, two men — sentries who had been patrolling the woods — came around a corner. It was hard to tell who was more surprised to see whom, and they'd barely let out a shout when one of the vigilantes pulled a pistol and killed the two sentries. Seconds later, doors opened and men in pajamas holding lanterns poured into the streets. Women and children huddled behind them in fear.

Fueled by liquor, a vigilante let out a whoop and shot five more men. The confused people screamed and ran everywhere. But that wasn't the worst of it. In the blink of an eye, things literally went to hell.

One raider, a laborer named Auguste Dauphin, grabbed a young girl by the hair, dragged her to the ground, and ripped off her nightshirt. He unbuckled his belt, dropped his pants, and yelled, "Let's see how a woman acts when the devil's inside her!" She screamed in pain as he mounted her. Afraid of the now-enraged cult members who moved closer, his four friends held their guns on the crowd and ordered them back.

"Auguste! What the hell have you done?" David Hebert screamed. "This isn't what we're here for!" But he didn't go to the girl's side. He didn't pull Auguste off or try to help at all.

As unbelievable as it is to think Auguste would make things worse, it happened. He had defiled the girl in front of a hundred or more townspeople who would never forget tonight, but in his whisky-fogged stupor, Auguste became worried the girl might remember his face.

Before his friends could stop him, he picked up a stick and gouged out the eyes of the helpless, naked teenager. As her screams pierced the night, the other vigilantes jerked him up and told him to run to the boats. Behind them the infuriated cult members moved toward them like zombies — with slow, deliberate steps.

"Burn the place and let's get out of here," one terrified man shouted, and another tossed a match on the gasoline. In an instant several buildings were ablaze, and within minutes the town was a roaring inferno.

Firing shots over their shoulders, the vigilantes jumped into their boats and pulled away from shore. They were some distance away before they realized that one was missing. In their haste, they had left the rapist behind. There was no time to go back; they steered out into the river and began to row furiously.

Then came a bloodcurdling scream. With the tremendous fire as a backdrop, they watched the scene unfolding on the shoreline. One of the cult members held

Auguste in a vise grip while another looped a noose around his neck. Unable to help, the vigilantes in their boats looked on as townspeople grabbed their friend and plunged a stick into his eyes. Another tossed a rope over a limb, put a noose around Auguste's neck, and hoisted him up. He writhed in agony, and then he was still.

"Let's go back and kill 'em all!" one of the drunken criminals yelled, but the others wouldn't let it happen. Auguste deserved what he had gotten, and if they went back, they would meet the same fate.

They looked back just before they rounded a bend, and saw a man standing below Auguste's swaying body. Grinning from ear to ear, he waved to them as he twirled the corpse around and around, and he whistled a tune that wafted across the still water. It was an eerie sound, something like the warble of a whip-poor-will, that would haunt them as an eternal reminder of the horrors they committed that night.

They docked at Abbeville around daybreak and went home to panic-stricken wives who demanded they reveal where they'd been. The women got nothing; their husbands fell into alcohol-fueled comas and awoke with memories of terrifying nightmares. Then they realized those weren't dreams at all. They had done those things, and they had left Auguste at the scene of the crime.

Those four vigilantes met the next day, swore an oath, and promised never to reveal what they had done. Three of the four got away with it, although they would say they never escaped the memories. The fourth — my great-grandfather Simon Navarro — was not so fortunate. A smuggler and rumrunner who plied his trade on the river, he made a huge mistake he likely never realized. He ran a load of whisky the night of May 26, 1890, the tenth anniversary of the debacle at Asher.

He saw bonfires on the shore, but perhaps he didn't realize just where he was along the river. Maybe it was a cult member who recognized him. I'll never know exactly what happened, but my great-grandfather disappeared.

I said earlier that I would explain how I know these things. Many families have long-buried secrets and relatives who were horse thieves or bank robbers or worse. But most of those families have learned to live with it. They accept things they can't change, laugh it off, and move on.

Some families do that, but our four families never did, for a variety of reasons. Influential politicians, rich people, pillars of a community, and even parish sheriffs believe they have good reason to hide the evil in their pasts. The four men who returned from Asher formed a Conclave, a group that met when necessary to suppress rumors, deflect those who were getting close to the truth, and protect their reputations. Auguste's family wasn't part of the Conclave because both he and his wife disappeared.

The Conclave remained active through succeeding generations. Sons and nephews, and their sons and nephews, became guardians of the secret, and it still exists today. One hundred and thirty-nine years after the crimes occurred, four men still keep the awful deeds hidden. I know this because I'm one of them.

Junior paused the recording and glanced at Landry. "Here's where you come into the picture. You were the first person to come nosing around the parish that I couldn't warn off. I knew the minute I saw you in my office that everything was about to blow up. It bothered me at the time because I had followed the Conclave leader's orders. But I decided if it wasn't you, it'd be a different person on a different day. We couldn't keep the secret forever."

He turned the recorder on again.

I watched Landry Drake's crew open the graves because I wanted to know if my great-grandfather Simon's body was there. I thought the cult had captured and killed him, but I needed proof. The diggers found the bodies of two adult men, and I didn't need DNA tests to tell me who they were. One was my relative and the other Auguste Dauphin. Both had their eyes gouged out, like Auguste had done to that poor girl. An eye for an eye, I thought to myself.

When I met Landry Drake in my office, I worried about what he'd uncover. I'd hidden so much for so long, I didn't think I could come clean, but now at last, this is my confession. Forgive me, Father, for I have sinned.

CHAPTER FORTY-FOUR

Junior's confession astounded Channel Nine's director, as did Landry's experiences in Vermilion Parish. The director considered this story too full of bombshells for just one episode. It would air as a two-part series called *Billy Whistler*.

At first Junior didn't want his confession aired, but Landry pressured him to come clean before the world. He agreed, and Landry requested a few more answers. Who belonged to the Conclave today, and why did it still matter after so many years? Why didn't they step forward and simply admit they'd covered up crimes, but ones committed by others? Landry believed people would understand.

Junior disagreed. People would never understand because there was much more to all this.

As the last floodgates opened, the disclosures astonished Landry.

The Conclave consisted of four co-conspirators. He was one, along with David Hebert, a respected fourth-generation Abbeville funeral director, and Joel Morin, a timber magnate and one of Louisiana's wealthiest men.

Landry knew Hebert; along with Junior, he urged Landry to get out of Vermilion Parish.

The fourth member was the state's popular governor Waymon Ferrara. His campaign for a second term was in full swing, with the election in fourteen months. Disclosing his involvement in all this could carry grave implications for him.

And then Junior hung his head and explained why it all still mattered.

————

Today Junior sat on a couch under hot lights facing three cameras. He'd done interviews at stations in Lafayette and Lake Charles about cases with a human-interest twist or when making an appeal to citizens for help to solve a crime.

Nothing he'd ever done could prepare him for this. He sat in the French Quarter studios of WCCY Channel Nine. He'd made the big time, in more ways than one, and when this episode aired, his life would change forever. It was a bitter pill, but he was ready.

The names came out one by one. Mug shots appeared in the background as Landry explained each man had refused to make a statement or give an interview. Only Sheriff Conreco stepped forward to tell the truth.

The names of the Conclave members came out in an order that created the most sensationalism. People knew about Junior's involvement from the previous episode. Landry revealed the names of the undertaker and the timber executive. Last came the biggest fish — the governor. Junior provided background and commentary on how, when and where the meetings occurred, and what topics they discussed. He painted Joel Morin as the evil, conniving head of their band of bad actors and the others as willing participants in a conspiracy of secrecy.

Toward the end of the hour-long documentary, there would be one final exposé, one final nail in the Conclave's proverbial coffin. Like any good investigator doing a TV show, Landry saved the best for last.

Junior disclosed that the Conclave bore responsibility for the deaths of fourteen other people — each a teenaged girl and each on Remembering Day. On that awful night every decade, the reigning elder allowed a horribly misshapen inbred creature — a rougarou they called Billy Whistler — to capture, torture and murder a girl. It was a ritual in remembrance of and as a retaliation for the rape and blinding of the girl in 1880.

The sad truth was that if the vigilantes had confessed their crimes and faced justice back then, fourteen more might not have been murdered.

The bodies of only three girls had ever turned up; the other eleven were missing until Landry and the crew had found their graves in the Asher Cemetery. Now families could at last have peace, and beloved children could rest in family plots alongside their loved ones.

Junior allowed himself to be accountable at last, and his confession brought listeners to tears. Outraged viewers responded with thousands of tweets, posts and even death threats.

Junior continued. *You could say we have no complicity in something that happened so long ago, but like so much else we hid, that's a lie too. Over the years Conclave members have died off, but two have always been the same. There's always been the sheriff and the undertaker. One was easier than the other — David Hebert's great-grandfather was a vigilante, and it stayed in the family. The sheriffs were elected officials, and they had to ensure their successors became sheriff too. It was hard, but somehow they pulled it off.*

Today I am the sheriff, and today David Hebert the fourth is the funeral director. We carefully steered distraught families in the wrong direction, lied to them, and misled them. We let them wonder what happened to their children. I knew where the girls had been buried, because I went there myself long ago. I knew, but I didn't tell their fathers and mothers. That's the sin that ultimately brought me to where I sit today. It's far from my only sin, but it's the one I cannot forgive myself for.

Landry gave a powerful closing message. Why did it matter today? Because over the years each member of the Conclave had pretended to be something he wasn't. They had held themselves out as solid, upstanding and trustworthy citizens when they were nothing of the sort. It would have been one thing to hide the past, but this was an active, ongoing scheme to deceive and to break the law.

In addition, it was grossly unfair to the Sons of Jehovah, despite how cruel and domineering the leader had been. That night the people lost everything they owned, seven of their men died, and one of the children was brutally attacked and murdered. They caught one vigilante that night, and they captured Sheriff Conreco's great-uncle ten years later, but the others walked the streets as free men. So did their descendants.

The recording session was the most high-tension, explosive piece Landry had ever done. When Junior left the studio, the crew breathed a collective sigh of exhaustion. This had been heavy stuff — a mind-blowing disclosure. No one could predict what the repercussions might be after it aired.

Two people sat in the shadows of the studio and watched the taping. One was Grace from the Vermilion Parish court clerk's office. Watching the TV crew at work fascinated her. She patted Cate's hand during the session when her boyfriend, Landry, made important points.

Once the episode went through editing and was finished, Ted sent a copy to Triboro's general counsel. Everyone was ordered to maintain total secrecy; this expose would be a ratings bonanza if the attorney gave his approval.

The lawyer sent a letter to the Conclave members that outlined Junior's allegations about their clandestine group. They had refused to give statements earlier, and they did so again. But this episode was different — publicizing these allegations held major implications for each of them. Their attorneys threatened suits for libel and defamation. The station would lose millions, they assured its general counsel.

Although this story was a potential bombshell, most media executives are reticent to release even a true story that would cost them legal fees and perhaps a hefty settlement. But there are First Amendment rights, a duty to give the public the truth, and a capitalistic motivation that some stories are too potentially profitable to quash.

The three attorneys ranted about multimillion-dollar lawsuits, but what they *didn't* say gave Landry his episode. Nobody claimed that the information was false.

By their silence, Landry knew there was a Conclave, these men were members, and their long-dead relatives did some awful things one May night in 1880. In a claim for slander or defamation, truth is the ultimate defense.

CHAPTER FORTY-FIVE

Six weeks later

Joel Morin sat on his patio and looked at the sunset over Vermilion Bay. He forced out the rage because his blood pressure was too high already, and his doctor said stress could kill him.

First there had been the initial news reports from New Asher, the story of Landry Drake and his band of merry men who saved the cult and the world from disaster. That information was bad enough because Junior Conreco had been involved. He'd been there too, but he had betrayed them. Joel wished when the cult captured him, they'd killed him and been done with it. It would make things simpler.

More bad news followed. Teasers on Channel Nine fueled excitement about an upcoming Thursday evening prime-time special full of secrets and suspense. Its name was "The Cult and Billy Whistler."

He watched the show, which turned out to be nothing more than an hour-long recap of the original news story. It began with how the Sons of Jehovah captured the sheriff of

Vermilion Parish. WCCY investigative reporter Landry Drake and cameraman Phil Vandegriff had been working on a story, and they were on hand when the kidnapping happened. Phil's phone rested in a front strap of his vest, connected as always to a charger. He captured everything — the cemetery, the forced march, Em's imprisonment in a dog cage, the suicide of the leader, and the incredible Billy Whistler episode.

The video's grainy quality seemed spookier because it was slightly out of focus, and the audio filled with shouts and noise allowed viewers to feel the tension.

Veteran Channel Nine anchor Ken Spearman interviewed Landry, Phil, the parish medical examiner and Father Paul. Because of her fragile emotions, Em was spared. Neither her name nor picture were part of the show.

Junior wasn't there either, but Landry praised his actions, calling him a hero and a brave man who helped save others.

The documentary generated unprecedented ratings for the station. People across the country were enthralled as Landry told about how the cult leader kidnapped Junior Conreco, the subsequent battle and the death of an actual rougarou named Billy Whistler.

What raised Joel Morin's blood pressure wasn't so much the revelations of that show, but the chance that Landry Drake knew even more. Things about the Conclave, for instance.

Joel had been furious, and he called Junior the moment the show ended. He berated the man for five minutes, calling him a dimwitted idiot and warning him to be careful what he revealed to others. Junior was a part of the Conclave, like it or not. If he hurt them, he hurt himself.

Junior didn't speak during the call except to utter the word no. That had come when the chairman commanded him to appear before the Conclave and answer for his actions. Joel told the sheriff he would regret it if he shared any of the Conclave's secrets. At that point, Junior hung up on him. No one ever hung up on Joel Morin.

Joel called a meeting of the Conclave. It was ironic that this time would have been Junior's turn to host the gathering.

He called the governor's private line first. His schedule was always hard to work around, but he agreed to meet the next afternoon at the mansion in Baton Rouge. He had a dinner that evening, but he carved out an hour at five.

David Hebert accepted without hesitation. He was nervous and anxious to talk to the others, because things were getting out of control.

At the governor's mansion, the three men dispensed with the traditional drinks and small talk. There was little time and much to discuss. Joel called the meeting to order and said they had to decide what they would do about Junior.

"I'm sure you all saw the episode on TV. Junior got his fifteen minutes of fame as the cult's captive. That's all over now. I called him after the show, and I assured him if he hurts any one of us, he hurts himself as well. As long as he keeps quiet, I say leave him alone."

Astounded, the governor said, "Are you serious? Junior gave the reporter information about us. You're aware of that; all of our lawyers got the same call."

"I am aware of it. And *you* are aware our attorneys threatened to sue Channel Nine for tens of millions. They don't dare broadcast a show about the Conclave. They'll be out of business if they do."

Understanding now, Ferrara shook his head. "You don't understand. You haven't heard the news in the past hour because you were on the road driving up here."

Nervous, David said, "I was driving too. What was on the news? What happened?"

"The second episode will run on Channel Nine a week from Thursday. It's called 'The Conclave: How four

Louisiana families hid their horrific crimes for generations.'"

"Holy shit," David said.

"We have to kill him," Joel muttered. "I'll hire someone."

The governor jumped to his feet and roared, "You imbecile! Killing him won't help. He's already told his story. Your money can't fix things this time. You always made fun of the sheriff and David here for being stupid, but you're the dimwitted one. After the show airs, things will never be the same for any of us, Junior included. This is where it all ends, my friends."

CHAPTER FORTY-SIX

The explosive *Bayou Hauntings* episode garnered the highest viewership in the station's history. Landry was known as the ghost hunter, but this story proved he was a bona fide investigative reporter. Ultimately it would give him his first journalistic award.

The four Conclave members' lives were affected in different ways. Because he divulged the group's secrets, some called Junior Conreco a hero. Others said he was a despicable excuse for a sheriff. He'd gone through enough hell, and he didn't stand for reelection. He took a cushy job as the constable of the tiny resort town of Rosemary Beach, Florida, where nobody recognized him or cared about his past.

Joel Morin's wealth and timber business continued to prosper, but the undertaker David Hebert saw his business suffer. People in Abbeville whispered behind his back about how snooty he'd always acted, but in reality, he was hiding a dark family secret. Within a year he sold his funeral home to a national chain and moved to Georgia.

Until the story broke, most considered Governor Ferrara's second term to be a *fait accompli.* He faced no primary opponents and was expected to easily win his second term. But politics is full of opportunity-seekers willing to take advantage of the misfortune of others. Just weeks after Landry's documentary aired, six candidates had announced for Ferrara's seat. In November he would finish a distant second and leave office in disgrace.

———

Elder Abner Savary struggled to keep the cult together, but the Sons of Jehovah faced a new problem when the TV show aired. The cult owned the old town of Asher, but when they moved, they had established their new home on a few of the thousands of acres owned by the state of Louisiana. People in Vermilion Parish learned there was a cult in the woods nearby, and they raised a stink with their legislators. The Sons of Jehovah received an eviction notice.

Most of the cultists decided to leave, and they spread far and wide. With so many followers gone, Elder Abner's cult fell apart within a year. All of them would need mental treatment, and the Strange Ones needed far more than that. The fortunate ones got help, but others resorted to begging or stealing and ended up in jail, the last place any of them should have been after the lives they had endured.

Father Paul left the ministry. He had taken a human life, and as justifiable as it was, he couldn't stay in the priesthood. He went to New Orleans and joined the staff of a parochial school. At nineteen, Em became the oldest first-grader in the school's history, and she would continue to grow in social skills and her education. Father Paul would be her mentor and friend for the rest of her life.

———

After a quiet lunch at Kingfish, Cate and Landry walked hand in hand through the back streets of the Quarter, talking once more about their future together.

Things were even more uncertain now that Landry's career had literally exploded. The only certainty was whatever lay ahead, there would be a future.

They strolled over to the house on Dumaine Street. "Want to come in?" Landry asked, and she said yes. After all, the old man's potion had saved her boyfriend's life.

They rang the doorbell and the same two eyes peeped from behind a curtain. A lock turned and the same old black man stood aside without saying a word as they entered.

"It worked, mon," he said almost to himself, and Landry asked if he'd seen the documentary on TV.

"Ain't got a TV. Don't need a TV to know that it worked, 'cause here you stand."

"What do you mean?"

The proprietor cackled and showed his yellowed, snaggled teeth. "I know lots of stuff. It's my bidness. Good thing I reminded you to use the stuff, ain't it?"

"What do you mean?"

"You was about to die out there. That rougarou woulda gotten you if I didn't remind you to use the potion."

He remembered. He recalled seeing a familiar face — *this* face — when Billy Whistler was about to kill him.

"It was you! How ... how did you do that?"

"That's why the damn stuff cost so much. You gets technical support too." He laughed and laughed, and so did they.

CHAPTER FORTY-SEVEN

May 26, 2020
Remembering Day
Asher

Pete kept one hand on the tiller and guided his dad's aluminum bass boat down the Vermilion River. He kept the motor throttled down to avoid noise; he and Misty weren't supposed to be in the boat in the first place, and certainly not out on the river this late.

They attended the same high school in Abbeville; they'd been dating six months and she promised him a special treat if he'd take her to a place they could be alone. The first place that came to mind was Asher. When he suggested it, she laughed and shivered.

"It's a ghost town," she said, and he nodded, saying no one had lived there in a very long time. They would be alone.

He asked if she was afraid of ghosts, and she smiled. "Not if I'm with you, Pete. Let's do it!"

They hatched their plan and told their parents they were going to the movies. Instead, they drove to his dad's boathouse, tossed a blanket and a six-pack of beer into the boat, and headed south. The weather couldn't have been nicer on this late May evening — warm with a light breeze that helped propel the boat toward the abandoned town.

"Give me a hint what my surprise is," he said, and she turned around in the front of the boat until she was facing him. She undid the buttons on her shirt slowly, one by one until it was open. He was mesmerized. They'd messed around and he'd gotten to first base, but this seductive striptease was turning him on.

She removed her shirt, reached behind her back, and undid her bra. "What a nice night. Do you think I should keep this on or not?"

"Take it off," he answered huskily.

She did, and in the pale moonlight he watched her run her hands over her breasts.

"You like?"

He gulped and nodded. He could barely keep his attention on the river now.

"Want to see more?"

"Oh yeah."

"I want to see more too, but right now you have to drive the boat. When we get to Asher, you can see everything!" She put her hands on her waistband, unbuttoned her shorts, and pulled down the zipper a little.

Pete looked at the GPS on his phone and saw they were five minutes away. Thank God; he had a huge erection and couldn't wait much longer. A few minutes later they pulled in, and he tied off the boat. Misty left her shirt and bra behind, and her half-naked body entranced him. He spread out the blanket in seconds and they lay together, entwined in each other's arms, kissing and groping.

Suddenly she pushed him away and sat up, covering her breasts with her hands. "Did you hear that sound?" she whispered.

Given the situation, he wouldn't have known if a cannon went off.

"Listen! Someone's whistling!"

There came a warble, low and soft. It might have been from somewhere far away but maybe not. It was impossible to tell.

"Is someone here?" he shouted as wind rustled through the branches and some animal crept through the woods. The whistling had stopped though, and Pete considered that a good thing. He tried to pull her down, but she jerked away.

"I'm scared and I left my clothes in the boat! Get me out of here! I want to go home!"

"Shit," he muttered as he shook off the blanket and they walked thirty feet to the boat. He heard the animal again — behind them and closer now — and then there came an unearthly croaking growl as something tackled him from behind. Misty screamed and cried, her face a mask of terror as she watched.

Pete was strong; he played right guard for the Vermilion Catholic Eagles, but he struggled to get whatever it was off his back. It had an overpowering stench — a rotten smell like something dead — and its sinewy bare arms wrapped around his neck like thick vines that slowly tightened, suffocating him.

Whatever it was released its grip and Pete fell to the ground. Misty lay nearby on the sand, unconscious.

Pete was close to passing out himself. His throat constricted and he gasped for breath. He stared at the creature that had attacked him — a hideous *thing* with bony arms and extremely long fingers. It walked like an ape, its arms almost dragging on the ground. It was all muscle and it might have been naked — it was so dirty and the light so poor that it was hard to see. It crouched over Misty's body and began to whistle softly. Pete tried to cry out, but he couldn't breathe. He sucked in air and fainted from hyperventilation.

When he awoke, his throat hurt. He touched it and felt painful cuts. Misty was nowhere around. He called to her again and again, but there was no response. Then he called the sheriff.

As he waited, it terrified him that if the thing returned, there was nothing he could do. He sat in the boat and held an oar as a weapon. There lay her shirt and bra. How stupid he had been to come here.

Thirty minutes later there were bright lights on the river. Someone with a bullhorn shouted, "Sheriff deputies! Where are you?"

Pete yelled and waved, and a cruiser pulled up alongside Pete's boat. Inside were the new sheriff of Vermilion Parish and two deputies.

Pete told them all that he knew. They questioned him over and over, although they knew from Landry Drake's documentary that evil things happened here on May 26. Pete answered truthfully; his only fault had been bringing her here, something he would never forgive himself for.

They searched when the sun rose. It wasn't difficult because there was a trail in the dirt where something had been dragged. They walked through Asher and found Misty's body in a graveyard deep in the woods. Her eyes had been gouged out.

———

Landry hadn't spoken to Father Paul and Em for over a month, but when he heard the news, he called and told the girl what had happened.

He asked, "Em, how many Billy Whistlers are there?"

"Just the two."

"Why didn't you tell me there was more than one?"

She replied in her usual simplistic way, apparently unsurprised that Billy Whistler had struck again. "I didn't tell you because you never asked me."

MAY WE OFFER YOU A FREE BOOK?

Bill Thompson's award-winning first novel,
The Bethlehem Scroll, can be yours free.

Just go to
billthompsonbooks.com
and click
"Subscribe."

Once you're on the list, you'll receive advance notice of
future book releases and other great offers.

Thank you!

Thanks for reading *Billy Whistler.*

I hope you enjoyed it and I**'d really appreciate a review on Amazon, Goodreads or both.**

Even a line or two makes a tremendous difference so thanks in advance for your help!

Please join me on:
Facebook
http://on.fb.me/187NRRP
Twitter
@BThompsonBooks

This is book 4 of The Bayou Hauntings Series. The first three (Callie, Forgotten Men and The Nursery) are also available in print or ebook editions.

www.ingramcontent.com/pod-product-compliance
Lightning Source LLC
Chambersburg PA
CBHW031943110726
47902CB00001B/282